SAV

By Rar

Adult Reading Material

Cover art by Melody Simmons

Chapter 1

"I have to admit, Mr. Thomas, I didn't believe you'd have my money."

"I told you I was good for it, Mr. Golden," Cal replied.

"So you did. But fifty thousand is a lot of money." Jimmy Golden smiled at him.

Cal didn't reply and Jimmy gave him a thoughtful look. "You're a good looking guy. Isn't he good looking, Jax?"

"Yes, sir."

Cal's eyes flickered to the man standing just to the left of Jimmy. He was shorter than Cal but he was at least six feet and his scarred face and dark suit made him appear dangerous.

"This is Jax Anderson. He works for me." Jimmy waved his hand in the general direction of Jax and Cal nodded to the man.

"Do you have any restaurant experience, Mr. Thomas?"

Cal blinked in surprise at the odd question. "I'm sorry?"

"Restaurant experience. Do you have any? Most young men have worked in the service industry at some point or the other. Did you?"

Cal shook his head. "No."

Jimmy leaned back in his chair and stroked the swell of his belly absentmindedly. "Do you enjoy being an escort, Mr. Thomas?"

Cal shrugged. "It pays the bills."

"Of which you have many."

Cal reddened. "How do you know that?"

"I know everything about you, Calvin Thomas," Jimmy said. He leaned forward and opened a brown file folder sitting on his gleaming desk. He perused it carefully. "You're thirty-three years old, you live in a rather dismal apartment in the west end, your parents are Darla and Bill Thomas, both retired. You have a twin brother named Courtney and a younger sister Melanie. You also owe thousands in personal credit card debt, a car loan and a personal loan. You're terrible with your finances."

Cal gritted his teeth and gave Jimmy a strained smile. "There are reasons for my debt that have nothing to do with poor financial choices."

"I'm sure," Jimmy said absently. "What do your parents think of your career choice? Are they ashamed that their son is paid to have sex with women?"

"They don't know," Cal said shortly.

"Interesting. What do they think you do for a living?" Jimmy steepled his fingers under his chin.

"They think I'm a limo driver."

Jimmy snorted. "Very clever. I suppose it explains the odd hours and late nights."

"It does." Cal glanced at his watch. "I don't mean to be rude, Mr. Golden, but I have another appointment to go to."

"Of course. So many lonely women, so little time," Jimmy replied.

Cal gave him a tight smile and started to rise.

"I'd like to offer you a job, Mr. Thomas."

Cal froze and then sank back into his chair. "I'm sorry?"

"I'm looking for someone to manage my restaurant. Well, it's more of a restaurant/night club, really. My manager recently relocated and I'd like you to take his place."

"That's very generous of you, Mr. Golden, but I'm afraid I'm not qualified for the job. I have no restaurant experience, remember?"

Jimmy shrugged. "Let me be honest with you, Mr. Thomas. What I'm really looking for is a young, good looking man to deal with my customers. I'm looking to grow my restaurant business and customer service is everything. If I have you there, greeting the customers and attending to their every need, I believe it would be beneficial."

He stared thoughtfully at Cal. "As an escort, you've already proven that you're excellent with people. You're accustomed to providing top-notch service, and you're good-looking and well-spoken. Do a good job and you'll be rewarded appropriately. I believe in allowing my employees to rise up in the ranks, so to speak."

He glanced behind him. "Jax here, started out as an errand boy for me. Didn't you, Jax?"

"Yes, sir."

"So, what do you say, Mr. Thomas? It won't pay as much as your escort work – at least, not at first – but it'll be a steady job, no waiting for a woman to pick your face from a website, and one that you can tell your parents about." A small smile crossed Jimmy's face.

Cal cleared his throat. "I appreciate the job offer, Mr. Golden. Could I have some time to think on it?"

"Of course." Jimmy sat forward and closed the file folder in front of him. "Have a good day, Mr. Thomas. We'll be in touch."

* * *

One week later.

"Hold on, I'm coming," Cal shouted as there was a second knock on the door. He dodged past the pile of boxes he'd never gotten around to unpacking and swung open the door. He blinked in surprise at the man standing in the doorway.

"Good evening, Mr. Thomas."

"Hey. Jax, right?"

"Yes. May I come in?"

"Sure." Cal led Jax down the crowded hallway to the small kitchen. "Can I get you a coffee? Beer?"

"No thank you." Jax stared at the dishes piled in the sink and the laundry and flyers on the small wooden table.

"Sorry about the mess." Cal cleared a spot on one of the chairs and Jax unbuttoned his suit jacket and sat down.

"Mr. Golden would like to know if you're accepting his job offer."

Cal sat down and took a drink of beer. "He didn't come himself?"

"Mr. Golden is a very busy man," Jax replied.

Cal drummed his fingers on the top of the table. "What exactly do you do for Mr. Golden?"

Jax straightened the sleeves of his jacket before folding his hands in his lap. "Personal protection."

Cal raised his eyebrows. "What would Mr. Golden need protection from?"

He knew the rumours as well as everyone else. Jimmy Golden might have appeared to be nothing more than a successful entrepreneur but there were suggestions that he was involved with smuggling and dealing drugs in large quantities.

Jax shrugged. "A man in Mr. Golden's position can have many enemies."

"Do you enjoy working for him?"

"I do. Mr. Golden can be a very generous man to his employees."

Cal ran a hand through his short hair. "I'll be honest, Jax. I don't understand why Mr. Golden is offering this job to me. I have zero experience."

Jax crossed one leg over the other and leaned back in the chair. "Mr. Golden has the ability to see potential in people. He believes in your abilities to do the job."

When Cal didn't reply, he sighed lightly. "This is a fantastic opportunity for you, Cal. Do an excellent job, show your loyalty to Mr. Golden, and he'll give you the chance to do very well for yourself."

"How did you start working for him?" Cal asked curiously. His eyes travelled over the thin scar that ran from Jax's temple to the middle of his throat.

"I was a troubled kid and teenager. At the time, Mr. Golden owned a chain of convenience stores. I was caught stealing from one of them. I was brought to Mr. Golden and he saw my potential and offered me a job working for him. I could accept the job or be arrested. Naturally, I accepted the job."

"No regrets?" Cal asked curiously.

Jax hesitated and a strange look flickered across his face for a brief moment. "No regrets."

"Are you sure about that?"

"Yes," Jax said impatiently. "Listen, all you need to remember is that Mr. Golden values loyalty above all else. Do a good job, show your loyalty, and there won't be a problem."

"And if I don't?" Cal asked.

"Then Mr. Golden will have me break your kneecaps," Jax replied calmly.

Cal's mouth dropped open and he stared silently at the man. He jerked in surprise when Jax suddenly grinned at him, revealing even white teeth. "Just kidding."

Cal shook his head and snorted lightly. "Nice."

"Are you taking the job, Mr. Thomas?"

Cal rubbed at his forehead for a moment. He had spent a great deal of time mulling over Mr. Golden's job offer. With Court refusing to talk to him and an uncharacteristically slow time at the escort agency, he'd had plenty of time to consider it.

He took a deep breath and nodded. "Yes. Tell Mr. Golden I'll take the job."

"Excellent, Mr. Thomas." Jax grinned again at him.

"Call me Cal."

Jax stood. "Mr. Golden would like you to start Monday. Be at the restaurant at four," he pulled a card from his pocket, "and wear a nice suit. This is the address for the restaurant." He took a pen from the inside pocket of his suit jacket and jotted down a phone number on the back of it. "This is my cell number. You can call me anytime if you have – "

"Cal, it worked!"

His front door slammed shut and his sister's voice drifted down the hall. She wandered into the kitchen, pulling off her jacket. "I got Court and Julie back together."

Cal stared at her. "You're kidding me!"

She grinned smugly at him. "Nope! I just finished dropping Julie off at Court's place, and I wouldn't be surprised if they're having sex right this very min – "

She broke off and turned a soft shade of pink as she noticed the man standing in Cal's kitchen.

Cal cleared his throat. "Mel, this is Jax Anderson. Jax, this is my sister, Melanie Thomas."

Melanie gave the man standing in front of her a quick once over. He was tall and lean with dark hair and bright blue eyes. His dark suit fit him perfectly, she suspected it was tailored, and there was a hardness to him that made her nervous. The scar running from his temple to his throat, didn't help.

"It's a pleasure to meet you, Ms. Thomas."

She realized with embarrassment that Jax was holding out his hand and she took a step toward him and took his hand. His voice, deep and raspy, was doing weird things to her insides and when his hard hand swallowed hers in a tight grip, she felt a tingle of lust sweep through her.

What the hell?

"Nice to meet you as well, Mr. Anderson."

She gave him a faint smile and tried to drop his hand. He held it for a moment longer and she wasn't sure what was heating her up more, the touch of his hand or the look in his eyes. He released her hand and the spell was broken. She took a deep breath and stared at the floor as Jax turned to Cal.

"Call me if you have any questions, Cal. Otherwise, we'll see you on Monday."

"Thanks, Jax." Cal walked him to the front door and Melanie collapsed in one of the kitchen chairs. She was trembling and there were butterflies in her stomach, and she took a shaky breath.

Get it together, Thomas. He's just a man.

"Who was that?" She asked, the moment Cal returned to the kitchen.

"I told you, Jax Anderson."

She rolled her eyes. "Does he, uh, work at the agency with you?"

Cal snorted. "God, no."

She hadn't thought so. She didn't think there was a woman alive who would take one look at him and purposely decide she wanted him in her bed. He was handsome enough, downright fucking gorgeous in fact, but there was something about him that practically screamed danger.

He was the kind of man who would look perfectly at ease with a gun in his hand. The kind of man who had rough sex with a barely-willing woman and didn't think twice about it. The kind of man who —

"Are Court and Julie really back together?" Cal's voice interrupted her thoughts.

She nodded. "Yeah, I think so. I talked with Julie and she asked me to take her to Court's. They looked like they were going to kiss and make up."

"Thank God," Cal muttered as Mel opened the fridge and grabbed a bottle of water.

She surveyed the nearly-empty fridge. "Do you have any money for food, Cal?"

"I'm fine," he snapped. "Did you tell Julie I said thank you?"

Mel nodded and dropped into the chair across from his. She took a drink of water and eyed him thoughtfully. "Who was that guy?"

"I already told you, Jax Anderson."

She snorted in frustration and took another swig of water. "Why are you avoiding the question?"

"I'm not."

"You are."

Cal cracked his knuckles nervously. "Fine. When I paid Mr. Golden back the money I owed him, he offered me a job."

Mel set her water bottle down with a thump. "Tell me you didn't take the job, Cal."

"You don't even know what it is."

"I know that Golden's a – a friggin' mob boss and you don't need to be involved with him!" She nearly shouted.

He rolled his eyes. "He's not a mob boss, Mel. Jesus, where do you come up with this shit? Just because a guy is a successful business owner doesn't make him the head of the mob."

"Don't start with me, Cal. You've heard the rumours like I have. Besides, the guy would have broken your legs if Julie hadn't saved your ass and given you the fifty grand you owed him, and you know it. You couldn't possibly think working for a guy like him is a smart move."

"I took the job."

"You what?" This time she did shout and Cal winced before holding his hands up.

"Calm down, Mel! Christ, do you want the neighbours to call the cops?"

"Cal, you can't work for this man. Listen, I know you're desperate for money but – "

"It's not just about the money!" He interrupted her with a sharp bang of his fist on the table. "Did you ever think that maybe, just maybe, I'm tired of being an escort? I know you and Court think it's a big joke that I fuck women for money but it isn't, okay? Do you know what it's like to have to fuck a different woman nearly every night? I know I'm not great at relationships but even I get tired of sleeping around. And I'm tired of lying to mom and dad about what I do. I worry every day that they'll find out and if they think I'm a disappointment now, what will they think when they find out I'm a damn escort?"

He stopped, breathing heavily and glaring angrily at her, and she reached out and squeezed his fist. "You're not a disappointment to mom and dad, Cal."

"Yeah," he muttered before looking down at the table.

She sighed softly and squeezed his hand again. "What will you be doing for Golden?"

"I'll be managing his restaurant."

She blinked in surprise. "Really? You don't have any restaurant experience."

"I told him that but he has faith in me. Is that so hard to believe?" There was a note of bitterness in his voice and she shook her head quickly.

"No, of course not. I just – I would have thought he'd look for someone with experience, that's all."

"Jax says Mr. Golden likes to give people chances. To give them the opportunity to work their way up. I'm just managing right now but who knows where I could be in ten years. Working for Mr. Golden could open up a lot of doors for me."

"So this Jax guy works for Golden?" She asked.

He nodded. "Yeah. Personal security."

"Surprise, surprise," she muttered.

He frowned. "What's that supposed to mean?"

"The man looks dangerous." She arched her eyebrow at him. "How did he get that scar on his face?"

Cal shrugged. "I didn't ask. I hardly know the guy."

"Cal?" Melanie gave him a hesitant look. "Are you sure you know what you're doing?"

"Yes," he said firmly. "This is a good thing, Mel."

He glanced at his cell phone. "Listen, I need to call Vanessa and tell her I'm quitting. Do you mind?"

She shook her head and stood up before giving him a quick kiss on the forehead. "Are you coming to dinner on Thursday night? Mom's expecting all of us."

He nodded. "Yeah, unless I'm working that night."

He caught her hand as she turned to leave. "Hey, do you really think Court and Julie are back together?"

She nodded. "Pretty sure."

"Good. He deserves someone better than that bitch Janine."

"Yeah, he does. Hopefully Julie's not like her."

"I don't think she is." He walked her to the door. "I'll talk to you later, Mel."

"Bye, honey." She kissed his cheek and frowned when he ruffled her long, dark hair.

"Stop it, butthead."

"Whatever, gator breath."

She stuck her tongue out at him and left.

Chapter 2

"Mel! Over here!"

Mel searched the crowded restaurant and smiled when she saw Court waving at her from the far side of the room. She picked her way through the tables and sat down with a soft sigh.

"Hello, Court."

"Hey, how's it going?"

"Good. Hi, Julie."

"Hello." Julie gave her a shy, nervous smile and Court took her hand and squeezed it gently.

"I'd introduce you two but you've apparently already met."

Mel grinned at him. "You know I can't mind my own business, Court."

Court smiled at Julie. "Our little sister believes it's her personal mission to watch out for us."

"That's nice," Julie said softly. "It's good to have family that cares. It's great you could join us for lunch, Melanie."

Mel studied the chubby brunette as she took a drink of water. Julie seemed kind enough but after the horror show that had been Janine, she supposed anyone Court dated would seem nice.

The waiter approached their table and the three of them ordered before Court sat back and ran his hand through his hair. He was dressed in jeans and a shirt smudged with dirt and he brushed absentmindedly at it as Julie gave Mel another nervous smile.

"Have you spoken to Cal?" Mel asked.

Court gave Julie a quick glance before nodding. "Yeah, I called him last night."

"And?"

"Everything's cool, Mel."

"Good." Mel smiled. "You know I hate it when you two fight."

She turned to Julie. "They bicker constantly but rarely actually fight so when they do – it's awful."

"Did he tell you he's working for Jimmy Golden now?" Court changed the subject before Julie could reply.

Mel nodded. "He did. I'm a little worried about it."

"Yeah, me too. I called him last night to see how it was going but he was at the restaurant or night club or whatever it is and couldn't talk." Court frowned slightly. "He said he would call me back this morning but I haven't heard from him."

"He probably just forgot."

"Maybe."

"I'm sure he's fine. I've heard the rumours about Golden as well but it's better than him working as an escort, don't you think? That job wasn't good for him. Desperate woman trying to find magic with a complete stranger who is being paid to – "

She suddenly stopped and stared in horror at Julie. "I'm so sorry. That was incredibly stupid of me and I didn't mean to imply that – "

"It's fine," Julie interrupted. She smiled at Mel but her face was a brilliant shade of red and she looked close to tears. "I'm not offended or anything."

Court leaned over and kissed her lightly. "It's okay, Jules. Mel sometimes speaks without thinking."

He scowled at Mel and she gave Julie an apologetic grimace. "It's true. I've got a big mouth."

"It really is fine," Julie replied quietly. She smoothed her long hair self-consciously before smiling at Mel. "So, Court told me you're a nurse?"

"Yes. I work at the Sturgeon in the ER."

"That must be pretty exciting."

Mel shrugged. "It's always interesting, that's for sure. What about you, Julie? What do you do for a living?"

"Oh, I, uh, I don't work." Julie's blush, which had just started to fade, flamed back to life and Court squeezed her hand.

"Julie's thinking of going back to school. Aren't you, Jules?"

"Maybe." Julie gave him a tentative smile.

There was an awkward silence before Court cleared his throat. "Are you going for dinner Thursday night?"

Mel nodded. "Yes. I'm working the night shift this week so I'll just go straight to the hospital from mom and dad's place. What about you?"

"We are," Court confirmed.

"We?" Mel frowned at him.

"Jules and me. I'm bringing her over to meet mom and dad."

Mel couldn't hide her surprise. "Oh, really? You're introducing Julie already?"

"Yes, really." Court gave her a pointed look as Julie stood up.

"I'm just going to go to the ladies' room. I'll be right back."

When Julie was out of earshot, Court glared at Melanie. "What the hell, Mel? That was rude."

"I'm sorry," Mel replied. "But, seriously, Court? You're introducing her to our parents?"

"Yes. I love her."

Mel twitched in surprise as the waiter arrived with their food. She waited until he retreated before giving her brother an earnest look. "Court, honey, you've only known her for – what – a week? You can't possibly be in love with her already."

"Well, I am. And she loves me."

"Did she tell you that?"

"Yes."

"Court, it's just – "

"It's just what, Mel? What's your problem? Do you not like Julie?" He frowned at her.

"I barely know her, Court. You don't either. People don't fall in love after a week."

He sighed and she smiled gently at him. "It's just that after Janine and what she did to you, I don't want to see you getting hurt again."

"Jules is nothing like Janine," he replied immediately.

"I'm not saying she is, but I just want you to be careful and – "

"You were the one who went to Julie and asked her to forgive me. And now you're acting like you don't even think we should be together," he said heatedly.

"I'm sorry. I don't mean to come across that way. I'm happy for you and Julie, really I am, and if she's the one for you – then I'll be supportive. But, honey," she gave him another gentle look, "you thought Janine was the one too, remember?"

"She is nothing like Janine," he repeated through gritted teeth. "Just give her a chance, Mel. That's all I'm asking. She's shy and she doesn't have many friends. I was hoping the two of you would become friends."

"I will, of course I will. But maybe just don't tell mom and dad that you're in love with her. You'll freak them both out."

He rolled his eyes. "When did our family start believing I was a fragile flower? Huh, Mel?"

"We don't think that. We just don't want you to get hurt again."

"Julie won't hurt me," he muttered as Julie crossed the restaurant toward them.

"Wow, the food came quick," Julie said in surprise as she sat down next to Court. She picked up her fork as Court began to dig into his lasagna.

"It's why I chose this restaurant," he said cheerfully. "I've only got an hour or so for lunch and they've got the fastest kitchen in town."

Mel picked up her own fork and dug into her salad as Julie did the same. Court did seem much happier than he'd been in months and she made a vow to herself to try and get to know Julie better.

* * *

Thursday morning Jax sat down in the chair across from Jimmy's desk. He handed one of the coffees he was carrying to Jimmy before sitting back and sipping at his own.

"Thank you, Jax."

"You're welcome, Mr. Golden."

Jimmy, studying the computer screen in front of him, took a drink of coffee before typing rapidly on the keyboard. "Did the shipment come in last night?"

"Yes, sir."

"Any problems?"

"No, sir."

"Good. Have Mulroney come see me for the drop location."

"Yes, sir." Jax hesitated. "If you want, I can tell him for you."

Jimmy looked up from his computer screen. "I'm sure you could. You're being helpful this morning, Jax, aren't you?"

Jax didn't reply and Jimmy sighed loudly before turning away from his computer. "You know I trust you, right?"

"Yes, sir."

"You've been a loyal employee for nearly twenty years. In fact, there's no one I trust more in this organization. You're like a son to me. But even family can stab you in the back if you give them the chance. Always remember that, Jax."

"I will, sir."

"Good. Now, how's the new boy doing?"

"Considering he has no experience, he's doing fairly well. The ladies love him."

A grin crossed Jimmy's face. "Yes, I have no doubt they do. I've got a good feeling about Cal Thomas, Jax. He's a man drowning in debt and desperate men are easily swayed. If he continues to do well over the next month or so, we'll look at bringing him into the fold. He's got a clean background and a man like him could be useful for some of my more special deliveries. Law enforcement won't look twice at him."

Jax shrugged. "The cops are suspicious of everyone who works for you, Mr. Golden. A clean record won't necessarily deter them."

"You may be right," Jimmy said thoughtfully. "I'm getting ahead of myself anyway. Let's give him a bit longer. He's not making nearly the money he made as an escort, and I have a feeling that sooner or later he'll be more open to the idea of making some extra cash."

"May I ask you something, sir?" Jax said politely.

Jimmy waved his hand at him as he took another drink of coffee. "You may."

"Why this guy? There's a hundred young, good looking guys desperate for money. Why choose him?"

Jimmy shrugged. "I told you, I have a good feeling about him. I see something of myself in him, just like I did with you. I know most people believe me to be cruel and uncaring but I would hope by now that you see me differently."

"I am well aware of your generosity, Mr. Golden. I appreciate everything you've done for me and – "

"Yes, yes." Jimmy interrupted impatiently. "I know, Jax."

He studied Jax thoughtfully for a moment. "I want you to become friends with Mr. Thomas. He'll be more inclined to trust me if you're in his ear telling him how wonderful I am. Spend some time with him, take him under your wing so to speak. Can you do that, Jax?"

"Yes, sir. I can," Jax replied.

"Good." Jimmy turned back to his laptop and studied the screen silently for a few moments before glancing up at Jax. "You can go."

"Thank you, sir." Jax left his office, nodding to the two men who were standing guard outside the room and jogged down the stairs. He strode out of the building and walked quickly down the sidewalk.

He had walked nearly seven blocks when a man in a tan suit appeared by his side. They walked in silence for a few minutes until the man spoke. "Did you get the location?"

Without looking at him, Jax shook his head. "Not yet."

The man sighed. "We can't wait much longer."

"I'll get you the information."

"Will you?"

"Yes, Agent Darvin," Jax snapped. "Just be patient. If I push him too hard, he'll kill me."

"You came to us, Jax. You said you could hand us Golden on a platter and it's been nearly four months. We know how dangerous this is for you. The FBI and the district attorney both appreciate the risk you're taking and that you came to us, but they need him to be there at the drop. He's been arrested several times before and each time his lawyers have found a way to keep him out of prison. We can't take the chance again of him – "

"Maybe you guys should be better at your goddamn jobs, then," Jax suddenly snarled. "Maybe get a DA who isn't so personally invested in this."

"It's her personal investment that's gotten us this far," Agent Darvin replied. "Without her, Jimmy Golden would be untouchable. Her pressure, her dedication to putting him in prison, has kept him from widening his distribution area."

"Has it? Because each shipment of meth he distributes is getting larger and larger."

"Have you seen it?" Darvin asked eagerly. "Have you – "

"No. But his inner circle is dwindling and he trusts me. He'll bring me in to the circle soon."

The detective sighed with frustration. "Jax, we need some kind of assurance that – "

"Johnson is dead," Jax said abruptly.

"Are you certain?" The detective blinked in surprise. "We know he's missing but - "

"He's dead. He was killed by Chan," Jax said impatiently.

"What? Why?"

"Golden's been moving into Chan's territory. He killed Johnson as a warning and sent his body in pieces to Golden."

The detective's body was nearly vibrating with excitement as they walked down the sidewalk. "That leaves just Mulroney. Do you think he'll bring you in as a lieutenant?"

Jax nodded. "I do."

"Good, that's good," Darvin said eagerly. "As soon as he does and you find out where the next shipment will be, you can contact me and that bastard is ours."

"He won't be at the shipment drop off," Jax said. "He's not stupid, Darvin."

"You'll have to figure out a way to get him there."

Jax barked harsh laughter. "He'll never go."

"If he's left with no choice, he might," Darvin said.

"What are you planning?" Jax asked.

Darvin shook his head. "Don't worry about it. As soon as you're promoted to his lieutenant and as soon as we get the information we need to bust him, you'll be living somewhere warm with nothing more to do but drink mojitos and stare at the beach bunnies in their bikinis."

Jax grunted in reply and quickened his pace. Darvin dropped further and further behind him and it wasn't until the agent had disappeared from sight that Jax relaxed. He rubbed wearily at his forehead before turning down a side street.

* * *

Cal opened the door to his apartment and stepped back in surprise. Jax, his hand raised to knock, was standing in the hallway. He lowered his hand and smiled at Cal.

"Hello, Cal."

"Hey, Jax. What are you doing here?"

"I was in the neighbourhood and thought I'd drop by and see if you wanted to grab a bite to eat."

"Oh, uh, thanks but I'm actually just on my way to my folks place for dinner before I head to the restaurant." Cal straightened his tie before buttoning his suit jacket.

"Another time, perhaps," Jax replied.

"Yeah, sure." Cal stepped into the hallway and closed the door. As they walked toward the stairs, Jax smiled again at him.

"Are you enjoying your new job?"

"Yes, I think so. I mean, it's only been a few days but it seems to be going smoothly enough. I haven't heard any complaints from Mr. Golden so I'm assuming that's a good thing."

"Yes, Mr. Golden is quite pleased with your performance," Jax replied as they headed down the stairs and into the lobby.

Jax glanced at the stained carpet and the water-marked walls. "No offense, Cal, but this place is a dump."

"Yeah, I know," Cal replied briefly as they stepped outside. It was just after dusk and Jax turned the collar of his jacket up as they walked down the sidewalk.

"And the neighbourhood is terrible," he remarked.

"It's not that bad." Cal shrugged as they approached a dark alley. "Where did you park?"

"Just down the street."

"I'm parked on First Avenue so I guess I'll see you – "

He stopped as two men wearing dark clothing stepped out of the alley in front of them. The smaller of the two was gripping a crowbar in one hand and the other held a long, sharp dagger.

"Step into our office, boys," the larger man drawled.

Cal glanced at Jax. The man's face was serene and he didn't hesitate as he stepped into the dark alley. His adrenaline pumping, Cal followed him.

"How can we help you this evening, gentlemen?" Jax asked as he unbuttoned his jacket and took it off. He draped it carefully over a garbage can before rolling up the sleeves of his shirt.

"Ooh, ain't you a polite one?" The smaller man sneered. He raised the crowbar in his hand and spat on the ground. "You can start by giving us your wallets."

"I'm afraid we can't do that," Jax replied.

The two men stared at each other as Cal cleared his throat. "Jax, just give them what they want."

"Yeah, Jax, give us what we want and no one gets hurt." The man holding the knife grinned at him, revealing a mouth full of stained and broken teeth.

"And we'll take that watch too." He pointed to the large, silver watch around Jax's wrist.

"This was a gift. I cannot part with it," Jax replied.

"Jesus Christ." The smaller man rolled his eyes. "Just give us your fucking wallets and that fucking watch before I beat your brains in."

"If you want it then take it from me," Jax said softly.

"Jax – " Cal began nervously.

"Fuck this shit!" The bigger man snarled. He nodded to his partner and they rushed Jax. Jax, his face calm, snatched the lid from the garbage can next to him and raised it above his head as the man with the crowbar swung it down toward his head. It hit with enough force to dent the lid as Jax kicked the knife-wielding man in the stomach.

Cal watched in stunned disbelief as Jax turned back to the smaller man and, with three quick and brutal punches to the man's face, dropped him like a sack of dirt to the hard ground of the alley.

The second man, clutching his belly, bellowed with rage as he staggered upright and rushed at Jax. He thrust the knife at him and Jax blocked it easily before kneeing the man in the balls. The man dropped the knife and began to sink to his knees, coughing and retching miserably. Jax grabbed him by the shirt collar and lifted his knee, slamming the man's face into it. His nose broke with a loud crack and the man screamed hoarsely as Jax released him. He vomited helplessly on the ground as the smaller man moaned softly.

Jax rolled the sleeves of his shirt down and picked up his jacket. "Come on, Cal. Time to go."

He left the alley and, with one final stunned look at the two men lying on the ground, Cal followed him.

"Holy fuck, Jax!" Cal grabbed the man's arm and pulled him to a stop. "I mean, holy fuck! You didn't even break a sweat! I think you broke that guy's jaw, and I know you kicked that guy's nuts so high up he'll be singing soprano for the rest of his life."

Jax laughed as he handed his jacket to Cal. "Hold this for a minute, would you?"

Cal took his jacket as Jax did up the cuffs of his shirt.

"Where the hell did you learn to do that, Jax?"

Jax shrugged. "I'm Mr. Golden's bodyguard, remember?"

"Yeah. I can see why."

He handed him his jacket and frowned when he saw the torn flesh and blood on Jax's knuckles. "You're bleeding."

Jax studied his hand. "It'll be fine."

"You should go to the hospital. Your knuckles are already starting to swell. You've probably broken your hand."

"I don't need to go to the hospital."

"I think you do, man," Cal argued.

"I'll put some ice on it later," Jax replied. "I'll see you tonight at the club, okay?"

"Jax, wait!" Cal tugged on his arm again. "Hey, why don't you come to dinner at my folks' place tonight? My mom's a great cook and she always makes plenty. Plus, my sister's a nurse. She can take a look at your hand for you."

Jax hesitated before nodding. "Sure, I'd like that."

Chapter 3

Jax followed Cal into the small bungalow. He hung his jacket on the coat tree as Cal shrugged out of his suit jacket and hung it neatly beside his.

"Mom?"

"In the kitchen, pumpkin!" His mom hollered.

Cal gave Jax an embarrassed look. "Yeah, my mom's big into nicknames."

Jax grinned at him. "Lead the way, pumpkin."

Cal rolled his eyes and Jax followed him down the hallway. Light was streaming out from a doorway to their left and Cal stepped into the kitchen. "Hey, mom. Where is everyone?"

"Your father's downstairs watching the football game, your brother and his new girlfriend aren't here yet, and I sent your sister to the grocery store to pick up some butter. I was sure I had some in the pantry but I can't find it anywhere."

Cal's mother was short and plump with graying, brown hair. Her back was to them as she lifted a steaming roast out of the oven. Jax's stomach growled softly at the sight and smell of the roast.

"How's your new job going, pumpkin? Are they being nice to you? Have you made any new friends?" His mother asked as she poked the roast with a fork.

"It's good, mom. I'm enjoying it." Cal gave Jax another embarrassed look as his mother wiped her hands on her apron and turned around.

"Oh good. I'm so glad that – oh, who's this then?"

"Mom, this is my friend Jax Anderson. He works for Mr. Golden as well. Jax, this is my mom Darla."

"It's so nice to meet you Mr. Anderson!" Darla said brightly as Jax stepped forward and held out his hand.

"It's lovely to meet you as well, Mrs. Thomas."

"Oh please, call me Darla." She grinned at him as she reached for his hand. She gasped loudly. "Oh dear, your poor hand! What on earth did you do to it, Mr. Anderson?"

"Two guys tried to mug us and Jax kicked the shit out of them." Cal grabbed a piece of cheese from the plate on the counter and popped it into his mouth.

"Language, pumpkin," Darla said as she examined Jax's hand. "This might be broken, dear."

"It's fine," Jax assured her.

"I thought maybe Mel could take a look at it for him." Cal popped another piece of cheese into his mouth and Darla slapped him lightly on the chest.

"You'll ruin your dinner, Calvin." She pinched his cheek affectionately. "And that's a great idea. We'll have your sister look at it as soon as she's back from the store."

The front door slammed and Mel's voice drifted down the hallway. "I'm back and I have the butter. I repeat, I have the – "

She stepped into the kitchen and blinked in surprise at Jax. "Oh, um, hi. Mr. Anderson, right?"

"That's right." Jax smiled at her and she flushed before turning her to mother.

"Here's the butter."

"Thank you, butterfly." Her mother kissed her cheek.

"Hey, Cal."

"Hello, Mel." He ruffled her hair and she swatted him on the chest irritably.

"Stop it."

"Butterfly, poor Jax hurt his hand after a couple of hooligans tried to mug him and your brother. I told him you'd take a look at it for him," her mother said cheerfully as she poked a fork into the potatoes bubbling on the stove. "Pumpkin, drain these and mash them for me while your sister looks at Jax's hand, would you?"

"Sure." Cal lifted the pot from the stove as Darla smiled at Mel.

"Take Jax to the guest bathroom. The first-aid kit is under the sink."

"It's really not necessary," Jax said. "I'll just wash it and – "

"Don't be silly, dear. Butterfly's a nurse and you really should have that hand looked at. You might have broken something," her mother interrupted. "Go on."

She made a shooing gesture with her hand and Mel gave him a tentative smile. "Follow me."

Jax followed Mel down the hallway. She flicked the light on in the bathroom and he watched as she bent and rummaged in the cabinet under the sink. She was wearing a tight denim skirt and he studied the curve of her ass as she pulled out the first-aid kit and straightened.

"Um, come on in and I'll take a look at it under the light," she said nervously.

He stepped into the room. The bathroom was small and he took a deep breath as Mel opened the kit. Her perfume was light and flowery and he tried not to jerk when she took his hand.

Although not as short as her mother, the top of her head only came to the middle of his chest. She was on the slender side but she had lovely full breasts that pushed at the fabric of her green blouse.

She studied his hand carefully before turning on the hot water. He rolled the sleeves of his shirt up and she washed the blood from his skin before patting it dry with a clean towel.

"This might hurt," she warned him before manipulating his knuckles lightly.

He didn't flinch and she gave him a tentative smile. "Well, I don't think it's broken but I'm not a doctor so take my diagnosis with a grain of salt."

He shrugged. "It isn't broken."

She arched her eyebrow at him. "Have you broken your hand before, Mr. Anderson?"

"Yes. And call me Jax."

She pressed a clean piece of gauze to the biggest scrape on his knuckle, holding it firmly to stem the blood still trickling from it. "I suppose that shouldn't surprise me. In your line of work, I imagine you're used to broken bones."

He didn't reply. Her soft touch was making not completely unwanted tingles of pleasure run up and down his arm and he was fighting a ridiculous urge to lean in and kiss her full lips. He snorted inwardly. Now was not the time to indulge in a meaningless bout of sex and besides, Melanie didn't strike him as that type of woman.

"Is my brother in danger working for your boss, Mr. Anderson?"

"I'm sorry?" He frowned at her and she sighed impatiently.

"I've heard the rumours about Jimmy Golden and I want to know if Cal is in danger."

"I didn't realize you were in the business of personal security as well, Ms. Thomas."

"Excuse me?"

"How much of your time do you spend babysitting your brother?"

"Asking a simple question isn't babysitting," she said hotly. "Do you not have any family, Mr. Anderson? Family looks out for their own."

"Your brother isn't in any danger," he lied.

She studied him carefully. "Why are you lying to me?"

He twitched backward. He had spent so much time lying in the last two years that he considered himself an expert at it. To have this woman so bluntly see through his lie made him incredibly uneasy.

"I'm not. Mr. Golden is a businessman, nothing more."

She made a very unladylike snort before removing the gauze and dabbing antibiotic cream on his torn and swollen knuckles. "Bullshit."

He grinned at her. "You seem to know an awful lot about Mr. Golden's business practices. I find that odd."

She carefully placed Band-Aids on the scrapes. "Like I said, I've heard the rumours. I'm not sure that Cal working for Mr. Golden is the best thing for him."

"But being an escort is?"

She shut the open bathroom door with a harsh thud and glared at him. "Keep your voice down!"

Her cheeks were bright red and she was glaring angrily at him and, once again, he was surprised by his desire to kiss her. He tamped down the urge as her hand tightened around his. "How do you know Cal was an escort?"

He shrugged but didn't answer and she stepped a little closer to him. "You keep that to yourself, Mr. Anderson. Our parents don't know and it would be devastating for Cal and our parents if they found out. Do you hear me?"

He nodded, fascinated by the bright blue ring of colour around her pupils. "I do."

His gaze dropped to her mouth and she licked her bottom lip nervously. "Stop looking at me like that."

"Like what?"

"You know what," she said. "I don't like you, Mr. Anderson. I want you to stay away from my brother."

He grinned again. "You don't even know me. And I told you to call me Jax."

He moved a little closer, no longer willing to ignore his odd and immediate attraction to her, and she licked her lips again before straightening her back. "I know you're dangerous and bad for my brother."

"How do you know I'm dangerous?" He whispered as he leaned forward. Her pupils were widening and he felt a thread of satisfaction when her gaze dropped to his mouth and her lips parted invitingly.

"It – it's not hard to figure out," she muttered.

"You smell delicious, Melanie," he suddenly said.

She blinked at him. "I – what?"

"You smell delicious."

He lowered his head until his mouth was only inches from hers. "I'd really like to kiss you."

He waited for her to say no and when she hesitated, he gave her a predatory grin and pressed his mouth against hers. She made a soft noise of surprise and his arm slipped around her waist as he traced the seam of her lips with his tongue.

"Open your mouth, butterfly," he whispered against her lips.

She moaned softly and when her lips parted, he slipped his tongue between them. He touched the tip of hers delicately, his hand tightening around her waist, as she opened her mouth wider.

"So sweet," he murmured before he pulled her up against his hard body and thrust his tongue deep into her mouth.

He swallowed her cry of surprise and took possession of her mouth, kissing her firmly and deeply as she gripped his shoulders and pressed her pelvis against his growing erection. He cupped her breast, kneading it gently through her bra as she moaned softly, and sucked lightly on her bottom lip.

It was ridiculous how badly he wanted to fuck her and without stopping to think of the consequences, he reached down and pulled her short skirt up around her waist. She didn't object and he lifted her and set her on the edge of the sink, pushing his body between her thighs and reaching for her panties. He curled his fingers around the waistband and yanked. The thin scrap of fabric was no match for his roughness and they tore with a soft ripping sound. He stuffed them into his pocket as she pulled her mouth from his.

"Jax, wait, I –"

Her softly-muttered protest died away when he cupped her core and rubbed her clit with the rough pads of his fingers. She moaned again and he kissed her deeply as he circled and pressed the swollen nub.

He was surprised by her wetness. She was so ready for him that it made his cock ache. Still kissing her, he quickly unzipped his pants and tugged his cock free. He pressed it against her warmth and her eyes widened with surprise as he cupped the back of her neck.

"I want to fuck you, Melanie," he whispered.

She stared mutely at him and he licked her mouth. "Say yes. Tell me you want me to fuck you."

He paused at her warm opening, his cock throbbing and his balls aching, as he waited for her rejection. She wasn't the type of woman to have sex with a complete stranger in the bathroom of her childhood home - he knew that as well as he knew his own name - and he was already steeling himself to pull away from her when she gave a short, brief nod.

"Yes."

With a harsh groan, he clapped his hand over her mouth and thrust into her. She cried out, the sound muffled against his hard palm, and he forced himself to stay still. He was larger than average and, despite his sudden and undeniable need for her, he didn't want to hurt her. Her pussy rippled and squeezed around him as she stared wide-eyed at him and he moved his hand from her mouth back to her breast, sliding it under her blouse and petting her gently through her bra.

He put his mouth to her ear and licked the curve of it. "You feel so good around my cock, butterfly."

"Jax," she whimpered his name quietly as her hands dug into his biceps.

"Tell me what you need," he whispered.

"You. I need you," she whispered back.

He smiled at her and her breath caught in her throat as he slowly withdrew before sliding back into her. She gasped, her pussy tightened around him, and he fought against the almost instant urge to come.

Condom, asshole. If you're going to come in thirty seconds like some damn prepubescent teenager having sex for the first time, at least put a condom on.

Fuck. A condom was definitely needed. He was reaching into his back pocket for his wallet when she suddenly thrust her hips against his. It tore a loud groan from his throat and she gave him a wide-eyed look of dismay.

"Sorry," he mouthed.

"Mel?" The loud burst of knocking on the door made her jerk and clench around his cock, and his pelvis arched helplessly against hers as he groaned again and fought the urge not to blow his load right then and there.

Cal knocked again. "God, Mel, what the hell are you doing to Jax? It sounds like you're killing him."

"I'm fine," Jax said immediately. He could hear the hoarseness in his voice and he cleared his throat roughly. "She's just cleaning the scrapes. We'll be out in a minute, Cal."

"Well, hurry up. Court and Julie just pulled into the driveway."

"Be right out." Mel's voice was strained and high-pitched and she squeezed her eyes shut when Cal spoke again.

"Mel? Are you okay? You sound weird."

She pushed frantically at Jax and he reluctantly pulled out of her. She hopped off the sink, her eyes widening when she took a quick glance at his cock, and hurriedly pulled her skirt down.

"I'm fine."

"Are you sure?"

"Yes, Cal!" She shouted.

"Fine," he said irritably. "Don't get your panties in a bunch."

Her face turned a crimson shade of red and her gaze dropped to the pocket of Jax's pants, as Cal snorted and walked away. Jax reached out to touch her and she backed away, her hands held up defensively.

"Don't touch me!" She hissed at him.

"I'm sorry, butterfly. I didn't – "

"Go!" She wrapped her arms around her waist and glared at him. "Get out!"

He tucked himself back into his pants and zipped up as she stared studiously at the floor between her feet.

"Melanie, we should talk about what just happened."

"No!" She snapped at him. "I – I need a minute by myself, please."

Her face was bright red and her eyes were watering and he cursed under his breath as guilt rolled through him.

"I'm sorry, Mel," he said softly as he reached for the door handle. "I'm going to go. I'll tell your brother that there was an emergency at the club, and I – "

"No!" She hissed again at him. "Don't you dare. Cal already suspects something. If you leave now, it'll only make it worse. Just – just go out there and act normal."

He nodded and slipped out of the bathroom, closing the door softly behind him.

Chapter 4

Mel stared out the kitchen window. She was elbow deep in warm, sudsy water and she absently scrubbed at the pot submerged in the water. Behind her, she could hear the voices of the others drifting in from the living room and she blocked out one voice in particular as her hands slowed their movements in the water.

What the fuck did she just do?

I'll tell you what you did. You just had sex with a very dangerous man in the bathroom of your parents' home and it was the hottest, most intense moment of your entire damn life. That's what you just did.

We did not have sex, she argued with herself.

Good point. You were interrupted just when it was getting good. You should definitely go find that lickable hunk of yummy man meat and finish what you started. Take him upstairs. How hot would it be to have him bend you over your childhood bed and fuck you with that giant cock?

Shut up! And his cock wasn't that big. Slightly above average, at best.

You keep telling yourself that, sweetheart, while I grab the measuring tape.

She shook her head and scrubbed furiously at the pot for a moment as her inner voice continued to yammer at her.

He's a great kisser. A seriously great kisser. Why are you wasting time scrubbing the damn dishes when you could be taking him home and showing him the time of his life?

She sighed harshly and continued to scrub. She had shooed her mother out of the kitchen, offering to clean up so that she could have a few moments of alone time, and her mother had been happy to oblige. Julie had offered to help but she had quickly refused, herding her into the living room with the others.

Slip him a note with your address and something sexy written on it. Leave him no doubt that you're ready to finish what you started, you little tart. Only this time — maybe use a condom, yeah?

Fuck! She groaned harshly and bent over the sink, taking deep calming breaths as her heart pounded in her chest. She hadn't given a moment's thought to using a condom. What the fuck had she been thinking? She was a nurse for fuck's sake and she wasn't a stupid teenager, she knew the dangers of unprotected sex. She hadn't been thinking, that was the problem. From the moment Jax Anderson had told her he wanted to fuck her, she hadn't been able to think about anything but how it would feel to have him inside of her. She hadn't cared that he was dangerous or a complete stranger, or that her family was twenty feet away. She had wanted his cock and nothing else had seemed to matter.

"Melanie?" A soft hand on her back made her jerk wildly and water surged over the sink to soak the counter.

She cursed lightly and mopped at it with the dish cloth as Julie gave her an apologetic look.

"I'm sorry. I didn't mean to frighten you."

"That's fine." Mel forced herself to smile at her. "I was just, uh, thinking."

Thinking about the fact that Jax has your panties in his pocket.

SHUT UP!

Julie leaned against the counter and smiled hesitantly at her. "Is everything okay, Melanie?"

"What do you mean?" She cleared her throat nervously.

"You seem upset."

Mel stared at her. It was ironic that Julie, a woman who barely knew her, had noticed something was wrong when her family had been oblivious. Of course, her father never noticed anything and her mother had been busy grilling Julie and Court about their new relationship.

"Yeah, I'm fine. Just a little tired."

"Are you sure?" Julie gave her another tentative smile. "I know we don't know each other very well but I'm a good listener."

Mel opened her mouth to repeat that she was fine and was horrified when she said, "I had sex with Jax in the bathroom before dinner."

"Oh." Julie's mouth dropped open and she clasped her hands together at her waist. "I didn't realize you knew him that well."

"I don't," Mel muttered as her cheeks turned red. "Tonight is only the second time I've met him."

When Julie didn't reply, Mel sighed. "I'm not a slut. I swear."

Julie shook her head. "I don't think you are and I'm not judging you or anything like that."

"Why not?" Mel asked bluntly.

"Well, I'm hardly one to judge after I paid your brother to sleep with me on our second, uh, date," she said honestly. "Besides, I don't really have a lot of what you would call 'world experience'. For all I know, normal women have sex in a bathroom with a man they just met all the time."

"They don't. Trust me, Julie."

She took a quick look at the doorway before groaning loudly. "I don't know what came over me. One minute I was cleaning his hand and the next minute he had me up on the sink and ripping off my underwear."

Julie's eyes widened and, blushing slightly, she said, "Well, he is good looking in an 'I could break your arm with my pinky finger', kind of way. I can see the appeal."

Mel gave her a dry look and Julie shrugged. "I'm not kidding. Women like bad boys, right? He seems pretty bad to me."

"That's the problem. I'm not a woman who goes after the bad guy. I like them stable and reliable and predictable, and he's none of those things."

"You don't know that," Julie replied. "You just met him, right?"

Mel shook her head. "He's Jimmy Golden's bodyguard, Julie. The guy is paid to beat up other people. Predictable and stable is the last thing he is. He's everything I stay away from in a guy. Hell, the last guy I slept with was an insurance salesman who took his mother out for dinner every Sunday. His idea of Saturday night excitement was going to a late movie instead of the early show."

"But how was he in bed?" Julie asked solemnly.

"Awful," Mel replied immediately.

Julie burst into soft laughter and, after a moment, Mel joined her. When their laughter had tapered off, Julie touched her shoulder gently.

"So, are you and Jax going to date?"

Mel shook her head. "Hell, no. We didn't even finish having sex. Cal interrupted us."

"Oh." Julie picked up a dish towel and dried the pot that was sitting in the dish rack. "Well, maybe that's for the best."

"It is." Mel agreed. "I don't want anything to do with Jax Anderson, it was temporary insanity that's all, and I want him to stay away from Cal too. Cal's got enough problems, he doesn't need to get involved in whatever it is that Jimmy Golden is hiding."

"Do you think he's hiding something?" Julie asked curiously. "Cal says he's just a business owner."

"Cal's being deliberately obtuse about his new boss," Mel snorted. "He doesn't want to go back to the escort agency so he's willing to overlook the rumours about Jimmy Golden."

She sighed and rinsed the pot of the soap before setting it in the dishrack. "I'm glad Cal isn't working at the escort agency anymore, he really wasn't happy there, but I wish he could just get a normal job like Court. Court's offered to hire him on with the construction company numerous times but Cal refuses. Court says he's afraid of manual labour but I think he just doesn't want to work for Court. They've always competed with each other, and I know Cal believes he'll be a failure if he has to take a job from Court. You know?"

"I do," Julie said quietly.

"Mom says I spend too much time worrying about my brothers. She says I need to let them live their own lives and enjoy mine," Mel said.

Julie shrugged. "I don't know about that. If you hadn't intervened with Court and me, we would never have gotten back together. I'm very thankful to you. If it wasn't for you, I'd be sitting at home eating ice cream and feeling sorry for myself instead of meeting Court's family and wondering if they hate me."

She paused. "Wait, that didn't come out right."

Mel grinned at her. "We definitely don't hate you, Julie. We, and by we I mean me, might be a little surprised at how quickly things seem to be progressing between you and Court, but we definitely like you. Mom invited you to her knitting club and that group is harder to get into than a locked vault."

Julie laughed. "I like your mom a lot. She seems really nice."

"She is," Mel replied. "And you'll know she really loves you when she gives you a nickname."

There was a moment of silence before Mel smiled at her. "So, Court said that you're an only child and both your parents are gone."

"Yes." Julie dried another pot.

"That must be very lonely for you."

She shrugged. "I have a best friend, her name is Mary, and we spend a lot of time together."

"That's good."

Julie bit at her lip nervously. "The thing is, my mom died when I was young and my dad was, well he was controlling and didn't let me do a lot of things, you know? Mary was my only friend and that's just because she doesn't scare easily and refused to let my father intimidate her."

She hesitated and then pressed forward bravely. "He's the reason I'm so awkward and weird and completely inept at social situations. This sounds terrible but when he died I was – was happy. I thought that this was finally my chance to really live my life. Only, I didn't. I spent six months doing exactly what I had done my entire life – hiding away from people."

"What changed?" Mel asked.

"I met your brother. I know how we met wasn't exactly conventional but still – he changed my life. I mean, he *completely* changed my life and I will always be grateful to him."

She stared earnestly at Mel. "I love him, Melanie, I really do. I know you're worried that we're moving too quickly but I promise you I'll never hurt Court."

Mel sighed. "I just – my brother is the first guy you've dated and your entire life has changed because of it. What if what you believe is love, is really just an overwhelming gratefulness to him? I know Court looks tough and he is, but he's also very," she hesitated, "sensitive I guess is the word."

"I know," Julie said. "I understand how strange this looks but I really do love him."

Mel gave her a searching look before sighing. "I'm sorry. I'm sticking my nose in where it doesn't belong again."

Julie patted her arm. "I like how protective you are of him."

Mel smiled at her before making a sudden decision. "Hey, a couple friends and I are going to a movie and dinner Tuesday night. I'd love it if you came with us."

"Oh, um, I'm not sure if I – "

"C'mon, Julie, it'll give us a chance to get to know each other better," Mel said encouragingly.

Julie hesitated a moment longer before nodding. "Okay. I have a meeting with my accountant at four but that should only take about a half hour or so."

"Perfect. We're meeting at Carl's Café around five for dinner. Do you know where that restaurant is?"

"I can find it." Julie smiled at her. "Thanks, Mel."

"Thanks for not judging me."

"Judging you on what?" Court had entered the kitchen and he wrapped his arms around Julie and kissed her throat before staring expectantly at Mel.

"My behaviour at lunch the other day," Mel said briefly.

"Oh." He squeezed Julie affectionately. "Are you ready to go? I've got an early day tomorrow."

"Sure, peanut." She grinned at him as he gave her a mock scowl and slapped her lightly on the ass.

Mel snickered. "Mum said when Cal and Court were born, she nicknamed Cal pumpkin because of his giant head, and Court peanut because of his really small – "

"Shut it, Mel!" Court gave her a pointed look as Julie bit back her laughter.

"It was nice to see you again and I'll um, I'll see you on Tuesday night," Julie said.

"You bet. Looking forward to it." Mel grabbed her purse from the counter and slung it over her shoulder. "Can you tell mom thanks for dinner and I'll call her later?"

"You're not going to say goodbye?" Court asked.

Mel shook her head. "No, I'll be late for work. I've got to run."

* * *

"I don't mind staying at your place, Jules," Court said as they entered his apartment.

She shook her head and tossed her purse on the side table before kicking off her shoes. "I like your place better."

He glanced at the tiny apartment skeptically. "Yeah, it's way better than a giant mansion with a cleaning service and a personal chef."

"I don't have a personal chef." She smacked him lightly on the chest and he grinned and pulled her into his arms.

"I know."

She rested her head on his broad chest. "Your place has nothing but good memories for me, Court. I love it here."

"I don't know, I've got some pretty good memories of your place." He wiggled his eyebrows at her. "Your bedroom and the first time I tasted your sweet pussy, in the shower teaching you to suck my cock ..."

She blushed furiously and he squeezed her full ass. "You're adorable when you blush."

She stroked his arms and stared up at him. "Do you — do you think your family liked me, Court?"

He nodded. "Yes, I know they did. Stop worrying, Jules."

"Right." She smiled tentatively at him and he kissed her firmly.

"Are you tired?"

"A little."

"Then maybe we should go to bed," he said innocently.

She smiled as he squeezed her ass again. "Maybe we should."

He led her down the hallway and into his bedroom. He unzipped her skirt and tugged it down her legs as she unbuttoned his shirt and pressed a kiss against his naked chest.

"God, Jules," he groaned, "you drive me crazy."

"Good," she whispered as she traced a path of kisses along his collarbone.

He threaded his fingers through her dark hair and held her head steady as she licked and nipped at his firm skin. His other hand slid into her panties and he cupped her bare ass before pressing a kiss against her forehead.

"Take off your clothes, Jules."

He shrugged out of his shirt as she pulled her shirt over her head and dropped it to the floor. She was wearing a black lace bra with matching panties and his cock swelled at the sight of her pale flesh.

"Fuck," he muttered.

"Do you like my new underwear? I went shopping the other day."

He nodded, his gaze dropping to her breasts, "I fucking love it."

"Good." She moved her hands behind her back and unclipped her bra before slowly pulling it from her body.

Court groaned under his breath. Julie was growing more and more confident each time they made love and he loved seeing this new side of her. She cupped her breasts, pulling lightly on her nipples, and he growled under his breath and shoved his jeans and underwear down his legs before stepping out of them. He nearly tripped and she giggled a little as she took a step back toward his bed.

He growled playfully at her and she sat down on the bed and leaned back, resting her hands on his bed. She lifted her leg and traced her foot across his chest and he ran his hands up her leg. She sighed happily and lay back on the bed as he reached for her panties. He pulled them slowly from her body, dropping them to the floor and placing a warm kiss just above the neat patch of dark hair that covered her pussy.

She widened her legs immediately and pouted when he didn't kneel between her legs.

"Court, please."

He grinned and kissed her inner thigh before running his tongue along the crease where her thigh met her pussy. She moaned and shivered with delight and he smiled again when her hands clutched his head and she pushed him toward her warm core.

"What do you want, Jules?"

"Lick my pussy," she demanded immediately and he laughed quietly before pressing a kiss against her wet lips.

"You've become quite the demanding little thing, haven't you?" He knelt between her legs and reached up to give her breasts a gentle squeeze.

She took his hands and they linked fingers as he bent his head and buried his face between her soft thighs. She squealed happily and arched her pelvis, rubbing herself against his rough stubble as he licked and nibbled at her wet and swollen clit. Her fingers tightened around his and he squeezed them back as he nipped at her pussy.

"OH!" Her back arched and her heels dug into his back as she suddenly came.

He lapped at her until she squirmed against him and then placed a soft kiss against her thigh before moving up her body and settling himself between her thighs.

"A new record, I think." He sucked on one swollen nipple as her thighs tightened around his narrow hips.

"I love how easily I can make you come, Jules," he whispered as she traced her fingers across his cheekbone.

"I love you, Court." She pressed a soft kiss against his mouth and he groaned and thrust into her.

She cried out into his mouth, her legs hooking around his waist and clinging to him tightly as he began a smooth, slow slide and retreat motion.

"I love you, darlin'," he breathed into her ear. She made a soft sound of happiness and he closed his eyes and lost himself in the warmth of her body.

* * *

"What are you doing with Mel on Tuesday?" Court asked curiously.

They were lying in his bed and Julie traced the hair on his chest as he stroked her long hair.

"She invited me to go for dinner and a movie with her friends."

He could hear the trepidation in her voice and he squeezed her lightly. "Don't be nervous, Julie. Mel's friends are very nice and you'll have a great time."

"Right." She smiled up at him. "As long as they don't mind social awkwardness."

"You're not awkward," he insisted. "You think you are, but I swear you're not."

"You have to say that." She poked him playfully and he squeezed her bare ass.

"I don't have to say anything. I thought you had an appointment with your accountant on Tuesday."

"I do. I'll meet them after."

"Did you make an appointment with your investment guy?"

She shook her head and Court sighed softly. "Jules, if you're going to apply for architectural school, you really need to talk to him about taking money out of your investments."

"I know," she said.

"Have you spoken to the admissions guy at the college?"

She shook her head and he frowned at her. "Why not?"

"I've been busy and it's a different time zone so it's hard to get a hold of them."

"It's not that big of a difference, Jules, and if you're going to find out what you need to do to qualify for the program, you have to talk to them before – "

"I'm really tired," she interrupted. "Can we talk about this later, Court? Please."

He paused and then nodded. "Yeah, sure."

"Thanks."

She turned away, curling up on her side, and a troubled look crossed his face before he pressed himself against her and cupped one breast. "Goodnight, Jules, I love you."

"I love you too, Court. Goodnight."

Chapter 5

"So, Julie, what do you do for a living?" Bev sipped at her coffee as Julie cleared her throat.

"Oh, I, um – "

"Julie is thinking of going back to school," Mel broke in smoothly.

"How exciting! What are you taking?" Tina asked.

"I'm thinking of going into an architecture program." Julie sipped at her tea.

"I didn't know we had one here," Bev said.

"There isn't. I'd have to move," Julie replied.

"Kind of tough decision to make when you're in a new relationship, huh?" Tina said sympathetically. "I imagine Court is encouraging you not to go."

"Oh, um, actually he thinks I should do it."

"Really? That seems kind of odd for someone in a new relationship."

Julie gave her a faint smile and Tina glanced at Bev before taking a drink of coffee. "So, Bev, how's that project at work going?"

Julie breathed a sigh of relief and stared into her cup of tea. Up until this awkward moment, the evening had been going really well. Dinner had gone smoothly and there hadn't been much opportunity to chat during the movie. When the others had decided on coffee afterward, she hadn't felt obligated to join them, instead she had been excited about it. Now though, she could feel her usual awkwardness creeping in and she stared miserably into her mug as Mel patted her leg under the table.

She gave Court's sister a quick glance and Mel smiled encouragingly at her before leaning in closer and saying quietly, "You're doing just fine, Julie. Don't worry. Bev and Tina both like you, I can tell."

"Thanks," she breathed.

"Hey," Tina leaned forward, "how's Tom?"

"We broke up two months ago," Mel said.

Tina blinked. "Why didn't I know that?"

Mel laughed. "I told you, but you were right in the middle of your fling with Arnie."

"Oh, Arnie," Tina sighed before grinning at Julie. "Listen, don't ever sleep with a co-worker, it doesn't end well."

She turned back to Mel. "Dating anyone new?"

Mel hesitated briefly, glancing at Julie. Letting Jax Anderson fuck her in her parents' bathroom certainly didn't qualify as dating someone but it didn't stop the image of his face from flickering through her mind.

"Nope," she said.

Tina glanced at Bev. "Why do I get the feeling she's not telling the truth?"

"Probably because Mel can't lie for shit," Bev said cheerfully. "Spill it, Mel. Who's the guy?"

"There isn't anyone," Mel said firmly as Jax's rough voice echoed in her head.

The two women stared skeptically at her but before they could grill her further, Julie said, "So, you're not seeing Arnie anymore, Tina?"

Tina shook her head and launched into the story of her fling with her co-worker. Mel sent a silent thanks Julie's way. She had spent entirely too much time the last few days thinking about Jax Anderson and she was angry at herself. He was bad news and she needed to stay far away from him and his ridiculously big cock.

"Melanie?"

She glanced up, hiding her grimace of distaste at the blonde woman standing next to their table.

"Hello, Janine."

Julie stiffened beside her, a soft gasp escaping her lips, and the woman gave her a brief, curious look before smiling at Mel.

"How are you, Melanie?"

"Fine."

"Good." Janine smiled at Bev and Tina. "Hi, I'm Janine. I used to date Mel's brother Court."

"We know who you are," Bev said curtly.

"Right." Janine turned back to Mel. "How is Court doing? I've been thinking about him lately."

"He's doing very well. Couldn't be happier," Mel said.

"Oh? That's funny because I ran into Stu a few weeks ago and he said Court was miserable. Said he was still really missing me," Janine said.

"He's not and he doesn't," Mel said flatly.

Janine laughed. "Well, we both know you never liked me, Mel, so you'll understand if I don't take your word on it. Besides, I've really been missing your brother and have been thinking of giving him a call. I bet he'd like to have coffee and get caught up."

"Don't bother," Mel said. "He's not interested."

"There you go again, Mel," Janine gave another tinkling laugh, "always butting in on your brother's business. You do realize that Court is a grown man, right? I can't tell you how many conversations Court and I had in bed where he griped about how often you stuck your nose in his business. I suppose if you had someone, you wouldn't be so eager to interfere with your brother's love life."

Julie watched as Mel turned a dull red and Janine's grin widened. The woman was stunningly gorgeous with perfect skin, smooth blonde hair and a tall and slender body. Julie wanted to shrink under the table at the thought that Court had gone from someone who looked like Janine to someone who looked like her. Instead, feeling an unaccustomed anger at the way Janine was speaking to Mel, she cleared her throat and said, "Hi there. I'm Julie, Court's girlfriend."

Janine's mouth dropped open and Julie forced herself to smile as the woman looked her up and down. She might not have the perfect looks and body that Janine had but Court loved her and thought she was beautiful. She was certain of it.

"You're kidding me," Janine said faintly.

"No," Julie replied.

"How long have you been dating?"

"Why do you want to know?"

Janine shrugged. "Just curious."

Julie stared silently at her and Janine cleared her throat. "Court and I used to date," she repeated. "I'm sure he's told you all about me."

"No, I'm sorry," Julie said innocently. "He's never mentioned a Janine to me. You must not have dated very long."

Janine's eyes widened. "We were together nearly three years."

"Really?" Julie replied. "Three years and he's never said a word to me about you. Weird, huh?"

Tina and Bev snickered loudly and Janine's face flushed.

"This is a joke right?" Janine said loudly. "He can't — I mean there's no way you're dating Court. Look at you."

"What the hell does that mean, you stupid cow?" Mel snapped.

"I hardly think I'm the one who deserves the 'cow' nickname," Janine huffed as her gaze fell on Julie again.

"You fucking bi – "

"It's fine, Mel," Julie said hurriedly before placing a hand on Melanie's arm. "It's hardly worth arguing with a woman whose best insult is calling a fat girl a cow."

She gave Janine a frosty look. "That's not very creative."

"How long have you and Court been dating?" Janine asked again.

"None of your business!" Mel snapped. "Get lost, Janine."

"You'd better get used to Mel being in your business," Janine said to Julie. "She can't keep her nose out of her brothers' personal lives. It's why Court and I broke up."

"Bullshit!" Mel shouted. "You broke up because you were fucking every guy who looked twice at you."

"Whatever," Janine said with a shrug. "You have no idea the true story. I suppose Court would have tried to protect you from the truth. He loves you, despite your inability to stay the fuck out of his personal life."

"Go away, Janine," Mel said. "And stay the hell away from my brother."

Janine smiled at Julie. "It was lovely to meet you, Julie. Say hello to Court for me, would you?"

"Of course," Julie replied sweetly. "What was your name again?"

Bev and Tina laughed loudly and Janine flushed again before turning and walking away.

"Bitch," Mel muttered under her breath as Julie slumped back in her chair.

"Nicely done, Julie. The 'he's never mentioned you' bit was brilliant!" Tina crowed. "There's nothing Janine hates more than not being the center of attention."

Julie smiled weakly at her as Mel placed her hand on her arm. "Are you okay, Jules?"

"Yes."

Mel stared at her worriedly. Julie was pale and trembling and she looked sick to her stomach. She touched her arm again. "Julie, are you sure?"

"Yes. So that was Janine, huh? She's pretty."

"She's awful," Tina said dismissively. "No one likes her, Julie, and you're way lovelier than her."

"Thanks," Julie said softly before glancing at her watch. "Listen, I'd better get going. I'm pretty tired and I, uh, need to get up early tomorrow."

Mel jumped to her feet as Julie stood. "Jules, just wait. Janine isn't – "

"It's fine, Mel. Really," Julie said quickly. "I had a really nice time tonight, thank you for inviting me. Bev, Tina, it was lovely to meet you both."

"Nice to meet you too, Julie," Bev said. "You'll have to come out with us again."

"I'd like that." Julie hesitated and then hugged Mel briefly. "Bye, Mel."

"Bye, Jules." Mel watched her leave, biting worriedly at her lower lip, before pulling out her cell phone.

"Who are you texting?" Tina asked curiously.

"Court," Mel replied. "Julie is, well, she's a bit fragile and I think Court should know what just happened."

"She didn't seem that fragile to me," Bev said.

"I think it was a bit of an act," Mel said distractedly as she texted Court.

She knew she was doing exactly what Janine had accused her of but she really was worried about Julie.

* * *

Julie dropped her keys on the side table and kicked off her shoes before hanging her jacket in the hallway closet. Her head was throbbing and she felt sick to her stomach. She hated confrontation and she could hardly believe the way she had spoken to Janine. That wasn't her style, but the anger over finally meeting the woman who had hurt Court so badly had taken over and she hadn't been able to stop herself.

She swallowed thickly. Janine might be awful but why did she have to be so damn gorgeous? She felt like an ugly lump of coal next to Janine and —

"Jules?"

She jumped about a foot, crashing into the side table and sending her keys and the pile of mail sliding on to the floor.

"Court! You scared the hell out of me!" She stared wide-eyed at him. "Wh-what are you doing here?"

"I'm sorry, darlin'." Court crouched and scooped up the wayward mail and her keys before placing them on the table and putting his arms around her. He kissed her firmly, sliding his tongue deep into her mouth as he rubbed her back.

"I didn't mean to scare you." He kissed the tip of her nose.

"Why are you here?" She repeated.

"I missed you."

She studied him suspiciously. "Mel called you, didn't she?"

Court gave her an uncomfortable look. "She was worried about you."

"I'm fine," Julie said. She walked to the kitchen and put the teakettle on as Court followed her.

"Janine's awful, Julie, and I'm really sorry you had to meet her," Court said anxiously.

Julie sighed. "She couldn't have been that awful. You dated her for three years."

"I didn't know the real her and I was – well, I was just being blindly loyal," Court said. "I loved her and I thought she loved me."

"Three years is a long time," Julie said softly. "I – I don't want to be clingy or anything but are you sure you don't still love her, Court? I'll understand if you have some feelings for her or – "

"Julie," Court slid his arm around her waist and cupped her face, "I love you. Janine doesn't mean anything to me anymore. I promise you, okay?"

She nodded. "Okay. I'm sorry. I don't mean to be so needy I just – well, we've never really talked about Janine and it was really weird to just meet her like that."

"I spent three years with her and she lied and cheated on me the entire time," Court said flatly. "She broke my heart and made me feel like I wasn't good enough. There's nothing else to say about her."

Julie put her arms around him and kissed his throat. "You're amazing, Court, and Janine is an idiot for not seeing that. Beautiful but an idiot."

"She's not beautiful," Court said. "She's an ugly person inside and out and I'm the idiot for not seeing it sooner."

He hugged her tightly and Julie rested her head on his broad chest. It didn't matter what Janine looked like. Court loved her and she loved him.

* * *

"Mel! You look stunning!" Julie gave her a look of delight and ushered her into Court's apartment.

"Thanks, you look gorgeous as well," Mel said.

She smoothed her dark green dress down as Julie looked her up and down.

"That colour is so pretty on you."

"Stop it, you're making me blush." Mel grinned at her before glancing up. "Wow, Court – nice."

"Thanks." Court's face was pale and Mel gave him a closer look.

"Are you okay?"

"Just fine."

"He's not fine, he has a migraine," Julie said sympathetically.

"Maybe you should stay home," Mel said.

"No, it means a lot to Cal for us to visit the nightclub. I'll be okay."

Mel nodded as Court helped Julie into her jacket. She was feeling nervous and unsettled at the thought of having dinner at Mr. Golden's nightclub, but she could hardly say no when Cal had called and invited her. Her parents would be there as well and she was determined to support Cal in his new job.

She followed Court and Julie out of the apartment and down to Court's truck. "Are mom and dad meeting us there?"

"Yep," Court confirmed. "Dad texted me ten minutes ago and said they had just left. We should hurry."

Julie squeezed her arm and gave her a small smile. "Okay, Mel?"

"Yes."

"Why wouldn't she be?" Court frowned at them as he opened the door and lifted Julie into the truck.

Julie just shrugged as she slid to the middle and Court helped Mel into the truck before slamming the door shut. As he crossed in front of the truck, Julie gave her a tentative smile.

"Maybe he won't be there."

"Yeah, maybe."

"Do you want him to be there?"

"I don't – I don't know," Mel said honestly as Court opened his door and climbed in.

She stared out the window as Court backed out of his parking spot and headed down the street. If Jax was there she would be polite and not think at all about what it had been like to have him inside of her. He was bad news and she would do the smart thing and stay away from him.

Chapter 6

"Damn, little brother, I didn't think you'd wear a suit."

Court grinned at Cal before clapping him on the back. "You said it was fancy."

Mel glanced around as Cal kissed Julie on the cheek. The club was smaller than she had imagined and it was decorated in dark red and grey. A bar, long and curved with a shiny wood top, was directly in front of them and rows of liquor bottles lined the shelves behind it. About twenty tables were scattered around the room, most of them filled with couples and small groups, and a small stage with an even smaller dance floor was at the front of the room. There was a jazz band, all of them men and all of them wearing tuxes, playing and she jumped a little when Cal took her arm.

"Hey, Mel. You look nice."

"Thanks, Cal. So do you. Are mom and dad here?"

He nodded. "Yes. Come with me."

She took his arm and followed him across the room to the corner furthest from the stage. It was a bit quieter there and she smiled at her parents as Cal helped her out of her jacket and pulled her chair out for her.

"Butterfly, you look so pretty." Her mom kissed her cheek.

"Thank you, mom. Is that your new dress?"

"It is," Darla confirmed. "Do you like it?"

"I love it."

"Thank you." Her mom turned to smile at Court and Julie. "Hello, peanut, hello, jelly bean."

"Jelly bean?" Court said.

Her mother grinned. "It's my new nickname for Julie. Do you like it?"

Julie smiled happily at Darla. "I love it, Mrs. Thomas. Thank you."

"Oh goodness, call me Darla," her mom said cheerfully. "How's that scarf coming along?"

"Good. I'm almost finished," Julie said as a waiter, he was dressed in a tux as well, approached them.

"Good evening. My name is Randall and I'll be serving you this evening. Could I interest you in a wine list?"

"Randall, this is my family," Cal said quickly.

Randall smiled politely. "Then a bottle of our best on the house is in order."

He unfolded Mel's napkin and placed it on her lap before doing the same for Julie and Darla. He gave a slight bow and disappeared as Cal rested his hand on the back of Court's chair.

"Are you going to join us, pumpkin?"

"I can't, mom. I'm working." Cal glanced at the door as a couple strolled into the nightclub. "But I'll check in on you in a bit, okay?"

"Sure. Have fun, pumpkin," her mom replied before picking up the menu.

Melanie scanned the room nervously. She was not looking for Jax, she told herself and ignored the trickle of disappointment when she didn't see him.

"Son?" Bill was staring at Court and Court gave him a strained smile.

"What's up, dad?"

"Do you have a migraine?"

He hesitated before nodding and Darla reached across the table and squeezed his hand. "Oh, peanut. You shouldn't have come tonight."

"I'll be fine."

"He had so many migraines as a boy," Darla said to Julie. "We were terrified he had a brain tumour but the tests came back negative and the doctors said it was stress that caused the headaches."

She squeezed Court's hand again. "What are you stressed about, peanut?"

"We're behind on a build," he replied. "It'll be fine. The client isn't freaking out," he hesitated, "yet."

"You'll get it done, Court," Bill said reassuringly.

"Thanks, dad."

Julie rubbed his back as he squinted at the menu before closing it.

"What are you having to eat?" She asked.

"I don't have much of an appetite," he admitted.

"You should try and eat something," Mel said. "I know you don't want to, but it might help with the migraine."

He nodded and opened the menu again as Julie gave him a worried look.

Mel took another quick glance around the club. There was still no sign of Jax and she forced herself to study the menu.

* * *

"I ate way too much," Darla said before dabbing delicately at her mouth with her napkin. "The food is amazing here."

Bill grinned at her, "I've always loved a woman with a healthy appetite."

Darla smacked him lightly on the arm. "Watch it, mister. You know I – "

"Did you enjoy your meal?" Cal was suddenly standing next to the table and Darla beamed at him.

"It was delicious, pumpkin. Thank you."

"Good. I'd like to introduce my boss, Mr. Jimmy Golden."

Bill and Court stood and Mel watched as they shook hands with the short, balding man.

"Mr. Golden, these are my parents, Bill and Darla Thomas, and my brother Court and his girlfriend, Julie."

"Wonderful to meet you." Mr. Golden smiled at them before turning his attention to Melanie. "And who is this lovely creature?"

Mel forced herself to smile at him as Cal said, "This is my younger sister, Melanie Thomas."

"Hello, Mr. Golden. It's a pleasure to meet you."

"The pleasure is all mine, Ms. Thomas." He held her hand firmly and she forced herself not to shudder.

The man had the looks of a kindly grandfather but there was a ruthlessness in his eyes that he couldn't quite conceal, she decided. She supposed that didn't automatically make him some kind of crime lord but it did make her extremely uncomfortable.

He released her hand and she refrained from wiping it on her napkin as he smiled at her parents. "I'm very pleased with your boy's performance here at the nightclub. He's done exceedingly well in a very short time."

"Well, he's always been a very quick learner," Darla said with a hint of pride in her voice.

"Indeed. I have big plans for your son. He possesses the ability to do quite well in the nightclub business," Mr. Golden replied.

"Do you have children, Mr. Golden?" Bill asked.

"I have a daughter. I had hoped she would join the family business but unfortunately," he hesitated, a brief look of anger flickering across his face, "we have drifted apart as she's grown older."

"I'm sorry to hear that. Children often need to find their own path, I suppose," Darla replied.

"Yes, I suppose they do." He glanced behind him and waved. Mel's stomach dropped when Jax Anderson materialized beside him.

"This is my associate, Jax Anderson. Jax, this is – "

"Oh, we've already met Mr. Anderson," Darla said brightly. "He came by the house the other day with Cal for dinner."

"Did he?" Mr. Golden said.

"He did. Hello again, Mr. Anderson," Darla said.

"Hello, Mrs. Thomas. You look lovely this evening."

"Thank you."

As Jax shook hands with her father and her brother, Mel stared down at her plate and willed herself not to blush. Jax was wearing a dark suit that clung to his broad shoulders and emphasized the narrowness of his waist and he looked ridiculously sexy. She could hardly stop herself from taking a quick peek at the front of his pants and she scolded herself fiercely.

Do not stare at his dick, Thomas! Jesus, get yourself under control. You act like you've never seen a man's dick before.

"Mel?" Her mother's voice broke through her thoughts and Mel gave her a strained smile.

"Yes?"

"Mr. Anderson is saying hello."

She swallowed thickly and forced herself to smile at Jax. "Sorry. Hello, Mr. Anderson."

"Hello, Ms. Thomas. It's nice to see you again."

"You as well."

He stared at her, his eyes seemed to pierce right through her, and she cleared her throat nervously before forcing herself to look away.

There was awkward silence and Mel gave Julie a frantic look as her mother stared curiously at her and Jax. Julie, her face flushing a little, broke the silence.

"Court, would you dance with me?"

Court's face was pale and he looked a little nauseated but he nodded. "I would love to, darlin'."

He took her hand and led her toward the dance floor as Darla watched. "Oh, dancing. It's been so long since we've danced, Bill."

"Well, I guess we should remedy that. May I have this dance?" Her father held his hand out.

Darla hesitated, her gaze flickering to Mel. "I don't want to leave poor Mel sitting here all by herself."

"It's fine, mom," Mel said. "Go and dance with dad. Have fun."

"I just feel bad, butterfly, leaving you alone at the table." Her gaze switched to Jax and she smiled sweetly at him as Mel bit back her groan of dismay.

"I'm sure Jax would be honoured to dance with your daughter," Mr. Golden said smoothly. "Wouldn't you, Jax?"

"I would," Jax replied immediately. "Ms. Thomas?" He held his hand out to her and, her stomach churning with anxiety, Mel forced herself to smile at him.

"Oh, I'm really not much of a dancer but thank you anyway, Mr. – "

"What? You love dancing, Mel," Cal said. "You took ten years of dance lessons."

She could have cheerfully killed her brother in that moment but she ignored her homicidal urge and took Jax's hand.

Her mother smiled delightedly and followed her father to the dance floor as Jax, his lean fingers gripping hers tightly, led her past the tables and on to the dance floor. She gasped when he pulled her up against his hard body.

"You're holding me too tightly, Mr. Anderson."

"You look lovely tonight, butterfly," he replied as he moved her smoothly around the dance floor.

She was a little surprised by his dancing abilities and he must have seen it on her face because he said, "You're not the only one who took dance lessons, you know."

"You're kidding me." She stared in surprise at him.

He shrugged. "I have a wide variety of interests."

She shivered when the tips of his fingers caressed her bare upper back. "Stop that."

"Stop what?"

"Touching me."

"We're dancing. I kind of have to touch you," he said.

"Not like that," she hissed at him.

"Have I mentioned how lovely you look?" He asked.

"Yes." She scowled at him.

He laughed. "You know, most women like it when I compliment them."

"I'm not most women,"

"No, you certainly are not, butterfly," he said.

"You don't get to call me that."

"Why not?"

"Well, because we don't even know each other and that nickname is reserved for people who are close to me," she said stupidly.

He pulled her even closer and her breath stopped when he dipped his head toward her. Her lips parted automatically and he groaned before clearing his throat. "I think fucking you in the bathroom makes us close, don't you?"

She flushed bright red and glared at him. "Keep your voice down!"

She stared nervously at her parents. They were dancing a few feet away and Jax steered her away from them as he grinned at her.

"You should be apologizing to me for that, by the way," she said.

"I never apologize for giving a woman what she needs."

"I – I didn't need it."

"Didn't you?" He asked.

"No," she whispered.

"So you didn't like having my cock in your tight little pussy?" He asked in a low voice.

She ignored the way her panties immediately dampened. "I – I didn't say I didn't like it. I just didn't need it."

"I did," he confessed abruptly. "Your wet pussy, the way you moaned my name – it's all I've thought about. I want – *need* – to finish what we started."

"It was a mistake," she whispered. "I don't – I don't date men like you."

"Who said anything about dating?" He replied. "Sorry, butterfly, I don't date at all. But that doesn't mean we can't have one night together."

"Charming," she said dryly.

He shrugged. "Honest. I don't want you thinking this is something it isn't."

"It isn't going to be anything. I'm not going to have sex with you, Mr. Anderson."

"You already have," he pointed out teasingly. "Why not take a night to finish it? I'll make you feel so good, butterfly. I promise."

"Someone's full of himself," she muttered.

He grinned. "You like my confidence."

"I don't even know you. Why would I spend the night with you? You're dangerous and – and bad for me," she said lamely.

His grin widened. "Let me guess, you've only ever slept with the good guys."

She didn't reply and he rubbed her lower back. "One night, butterfly. That's all I'm asking for. Let me show you how good I can make you feel."

"Mr. Anderson, I – "

"Jax."

"Jax, I – despite what happened before, I'm not the girl who just sleeps with someone she barely knows."

"I know you're not," he said.

"Then why are you asking me to do this?"

"I can't sleep, I can't concentrate, and you're all I think about. I want you in my bed. I want to be between those smooth thighs and deep inside of you. I want to hear you cry my name when you come," he said honestly.

She blinked at him. She had never once had a man be so direct with her about sex and it was making her hotter than hell. Her gaze dropped to his mouth. She could still remember how it felt to kiss him, how good he had tasted, and he inhaled sharply as his arm tightened around her.

"Keep looking at me like that, butterfly, and I'll fuck you right here."

"You would not," she whispered weakly.

He gave her a predator grin. "Well, maybe not right here but definitely in the bathroom."

She flushed and stared at his chest as he moved her easily around the dance floor. "What about Mr. Golden?"

"What about him?" He asked.

"You work for a crime lord. What happens if he finds out we slept together? Will it put me in some kind of danger?"

"I'm a very private person, Melanie. No one will know anything that happens between us."

She was tempted, fuck was she tempted. What harm would there be in one night of sex?

Plenty of harm, Thomas. Don't be fooled into thinking you're the type of girl who can sleep with a guy and then just walk away. It doesn't matter how much you want him or –

"Mel?"

Julie's soft voice spoke behind her. She was standing behind her and she gave Jax an apologetic look. "I'm sorry to interrupt, but I'm going to take Court home. He's really feeling awful."

Court was standing next to her, his eyes closed and his face pale, and Mel tried to step away from Jax. He tightened his hold on her and she gave him a frustrated look.

"I have to go, Jax. Court and Julie are my ride home."

"Mom and dad can give you a ride home," Court mumbled. "Don't leave early because of me."

"I don't mind, honey," Mel said. "In fact, I – "

He shook his head and then winced a little. "Stay and have a good time."

He took Julie's hand and she squeezed it lightly before smiling at Mel. "Do you want to stay, Mel?"

Mel hesitated before nodding. She did want to stay. She wanted to keep dancing with Jax, wanted to give him the chance to convince her that she should spend the night with him. Knowing it was madness but unable to resist the urge to stay in his arms, she patted Court's shoulder lightly.

"Go home and go to bed, honey. I'll call you tomorrow and see how you're feeling, okay?"

He smiled faintly and allowed Julie to lead him off the dance floor.

"I'm glad you stayed, butterfly," Jax said.

She stared up at him as the song ended. "I stayed because I want to support Cal in his new job."

"Of course," he said as he stepped away from her.

"Thank you for the dance, Ms. Thomas."

"You're welcome, Mr. Anderson."

She walked back to the table, entirely too aware of his hot gaze.

Chapter 7

"You drove the Miata?" Mel said.

Her dad gave her an apologetic look. "I'm sorry, Mel. We weren't expecting to give you a ride home tonight."

"It's fine. I'll take a cab back to Court's and grab my car." Mel drained the last of her wine.

After their dance Jax had, to her dismay, disappeared and she was feeling irritable and out of sorts.

Bullshit. You're horny and pissed because Jax is gone and you're not getting laid tonight.

Shut up!

"I'll give you some money for the cab," Bill said.

Mel laughed. "Dad, I'm not a teenager. I can pay for my own cab."

"Why are you taking a cab?" Cal appeared at the table.

"Butterfly got a ride here with Court and Julie and thought she could get a ride home with us. Unfortunately, we drove the Miata."

"If you want to stick around for another few hours, I'll give you a lift home," Cal said.

Mel shook her head. "It's already past my bedtime."

Cal rolled his eyes. "It's eleven, Mel. God, live a little, would you?"

She shrugged. "You know I'm not a night owl like you, Cal."

"I guess. Hey, I bet Jax would give you a lift home. I think he's about to leave."

"Oh – no, that's okay," Mel said quickly but it was too late.

Cal turned and waved and she groaned when she saw Jax emerging from the kitchen. He joined them and Mel stood hurriedly.

"Cal, I don't need – "

"Jax, you're leaving right?"

"Yes." Jax nodded.

"Think you could give my baby sister a ride home?"

"I'd be delighted to," he replied.

"I don't need a ride home. I can take a cab," Mel said.

"Jax doesn't mind, do you?" Cal said.

"No, I do not." Jax gave her a sexy little grin and she bit the inside of her cheek as he moved behind her and plucked her jacket from her chair.

"Ready to go, Ms. Thomas?"

"I really don't want to inconvenience you, Mr. Anderson."

"You're not." He turned to her parents and shook their hands. "It was nice to see you again, Mr. and Mrs. Thomas."

"So lovely to see you, Jax," Darla said. "Make sure you get my butterfly home safely."

"Of course." Jax helped her into her coat, his hands lingering on her upper arms for just a moment too long before holding his arm out.

"Ready?"

"Yes." She kissed her parents and hugged Cal before taking Jax's arm. He led her out of the restaurant and across the parking lot to a dark grey sports car. He opened the passenger door for her and she glanced up at him.

"Mercedes Benz SLS?"

He gave her an admiring look. "You know your cars, Ms. Thomas."

"My dad is a car freak."

She buckled her seat belt as he slid behind the wheel. "So is it safe to say I've impressed you with my car?"

"It's a bit on the flashy side for me. My personal feeling is that a man is usually compensating for something when he buys a car this expensive."

He laughed loudly as he pulled out of the parking lot. "You know I have nothing to compensate for."

She blushed furiously and his grin widened. "You're adorable when you blush, butterfly. Besides, I bought this car for its reliability and safety."

She laughed. "Of course you did. It does seem very reliable."

"What's your address, butterfly?"

"My car is parked at Court's place." She recited the address and tried to calm her racing nerves as Jax drove. The interior of the car was small and Jax was a big man. His arm brushed against hers and a tingle of excitement went through her. She ignored it. She was acting like a teenager with a ridiculous crush. She needed a night with Jax like she needed another hole in her head.

You should give him road head.

Her eyes widened, her face flamed, and she shot the errant thought out of her head like a bullet. Christ, she was losing it.

He'd like it. You'd definitely like it. Be wild and crazy, Thomas.

She swallowed thickly and stared blindly out the window. She was absolutely, positively not going to reach over and undo Jax's pants. She wouldn't lean down and slide that thick cock into her mouth while he wrapped his hand in her hair and urged her to suck harder.

Her eyes flickered to his crotch and to her absolute horror she could feel her nipples hardening as a slow burn of need started in her belly.

Thomas! Get it the fuck together!!

"Melanie?"

Sucking a stranger's cock was absolutely, positively, not something that girls like her did.

"Melanie? Are you okay?"

She gave Jax a blank look. "I'm sorry, what?"

"Are you okay?"

"Uh, yes. Why?"

"You look like you're going to punch something."

He reached over and took her hand. It was clenched into a tight fist and he soothed it open with his long fingers before squeezing it gently. She tugged her hand free of his grip. If he kept touching her, even innocently, she really would lose all control and give him goddamn road head.

"I'm fine. Just, uh, thinking."

"About what?"

About sucking on that delicious cock of yours.

"How you started working for Jimmy Golden."

There was silence in the car. She wasn't surprised. Jax didn't strike her as the kind of man who willingly shared personal information and he had already made it clear what he was interested in from her.

"When I was nine, my parents died in a car accident."

She studied him in the dim light of the car. "I'm very sorry."

He nodded, "My mother had a sister. She took me in."

"That was kind of her."

He laughed bitterly. "She was a drug addict. She didn't give a shit about me, and I spent the next three years afraid and nearly starving to death."

"Oh, Jax." She gave him an empathetic look and, without thinking about it, reached out and took his hand. She held it tightly as he stared woodenly out the windshield.

"When I was twelve, I tried to steal some food from the convenience store near my aunt's apartment. I – I hadn't eaten for a few days, she had spent all of the money on drugs, and I was starving. At the time, Mr. Golden owned a string of convenience stores. He happened to be at that particular one when I was caught stealing."

She squeezed his hand again as he continued. "I can only imagine what he thought when I was dragged into the back room. I was filthy, skinny, and terrified that I would go to juvie for what I had done. Mr. Golden sent everyone out of the room and told me to sit. He had a big plate of food just sitting in front of him on the desk – fried chicken and this heaping mound of potatoes – and I was nearly drooling from the smell of it."

He stopped at a traffic light. "Mr. Golden pushed the plate of food across the desk and told me to eat. I just stared at him, sure it was some kind of trick, and he told me again to eat. So I did. And it was the best fucking meal of my life. When I was done, Mr. Golden offered me a job."

"He what?" Mel gave him a look of surprise.

"He offered me a job. He said I could work for him, doing errands after school and on the weekends or I could go to juvie. I chose the job."

"You were only twelve, Jax."

"Yeah, but Mr. Golden saved my life that day. The money I earned helped keep me from starving and he was, well, he was good to me. He sort of adopted me, I guess you could say. Made sure I stayed in school, he always said that education was important, and he bought me clothes and supplies for school. When I graduated from high school, I started working for him full time."

"What did you do?"

"By that time, he had opened his first night club. I worked as a waiter and continued to do personal errands for him. I joined a local boxing club and learned to fight."

"Did you box professionally?"

"I did a few fights but Mr. Golden said I was wasting my talent so I quit."

"To become his bodyguard?" Mel said skeptically. "That sounds like a waste of your talents."

"I'm very good at what I do."

"I'm sure you are. But is that what you wanted for your life? Protecting a – a drug dealer?"

"He's a businessman, Melanie."

"Is he?"

"Yes."

He was lying. She shouldn't have known that, she barely knew the man, but she knew instinctively that he wasn't telling the truth. She sighed as he parked on the street outside of Court's apartment building and shut off the car. This was why she couldn't sleep with him. The man worked for a drug dealer and getting involved with him, even if it was only one night, was a dangerous risk. And she didn't do dangerous. She did stable and reliable. Always had and always would.

"Thank you, Jax." She reached for the door handle and he touched her shoulder.

"Maybe I should follow you home, just to be certain you arrive safe."

She laughed. "I'm perfectly fine. But thank you. It was um, good to see you again. Take care."

She slid out of the car before he could reply and slammed the door shut before walking briskly to her car. Every nerve in her body was screaming at her to take him up on his offer and she ignored it grimly as she unlocked her car and sat behind the wheel.

He's bad for you, Thomas. Just drive away.

She started the car and sat for a moment, staring in the rear view mirror at Jax's car. When he didn't move, she pulled out on to the street. He got out of his car, his face was a mask of frustration, and she watched curiously as he popped the hood. She drove up beside him and rolled down her window as he slammed the hood shut. He returned to the driver's seat, cursing under his breath when he turned the key and there was nothing but a dry clicking noise. Fighting back the urge to giggle, she smiled sweetly at him.

"How's that reliable car working out for you?"

He sighed loudly. "I suppose I deserved that."

"You totally did," she laughed. "Do you need a ride home?"

He sighed again. "You're really enjoying this, aren't you?"

"I really am."

He suddenly grinned at her, her breath caught in her throat at the sight, before sliding out of his car and slamming the door shut. "Yes, Ms. Thomas. I would be delighted if you could give me a ride home."

"Wait, you didn't plan this did you?" She asked suspiciously.

"Yes, I planned for my very expensive car to break down in front of a woman I'm trying valiantly to have sex with, in the hopes that it would make her feel sorry for me and perhaps throw me some pity sex," he said. "Is it working?"

"Maybe."

"Really?"

"No, not really."

"Cruel, Ms. Thomas. And here I was thinking you were the sweetest girl I'd ever met."

"Girl?"

"Butterfly?"

She laughed again. "Get in. I'll give you a ride home."

He climbed into the car and clasped his hands together like a schoolgirl. "My hero."

"I do what I can, ma'am," she said.

"Ma'am? Someone deserves a spanking for that."

"Actually, I prefer to do the spanking."

He jerked in his seat and she almost laughed out loud at the look on his face. "Are you serious?"

"Would it be a problem if I was?" She asked.

"No."

He grinned at her look of surprise. "What?"

"There's no way you like being spanked."

"Why not?"

"Well, because, look at you. You're all muscley and stuff."

"So, because I work out I'm not allowed to enjoy a spanking from a woman?"

"No, but…"

She trailed off and then suddenly scowled at him. "Tell me the truth – do you like being spanked?"

"Honestly, not really. But I'm also willing to at least try whatever a woman wants in bed."

"So you'd let me stick a vibrator up your ass?"

"Ms. Thomas, you are not at all what you seem. I would have bet good money that you didn't even own a vibrator and now you want to stick it up my ass. Maybe I should take a cab home before you completely shock me with your depravity."

She blushed. "One – every woman owns a vibrator and two – you're the one who said you liked to be spanked. Can you blame me for assuming you like other kinky stuff?"

"Butterfly, if you think spanking is kinky then you really must spend the night with me."

Her blush deepened. "I'm not a fragile flower, I've done kinky things in the bedroom."

"Oh?" He leaned closer and rested his hand on her thigh. "Do share."

"That's not a good idea," she said a bit shakily before pushing him back gently. "What's your address?"

He recited his address and she started toward his home. Her hands were shaking and her pelvis was throbbing with need. She shouldn't have flirted with him. God, she was being a right idiot, but this charming, funny side of Jax Anderson was even more difficult to resist then the 'I need to fuck you right now' version.

Twenty minutes later, she pulled up in front of the small, modest home in the suburbs. She shut the car off as Jax unbuckled his seat belt.

"What?"

"You're kidding me. This is not where you live."

"Of course it is. What were you expecting?" He asked.

"I don't know – a mansion on the beach full of half-naked women ready to do your every bidding?"

"That's my summer home."

She laughed and shook her head. "Seriously, Jax? This is where you live?"

"It is. Would you like to come in for a nightcap?"

"I don't think that's – "

He leaned forward, cupping her face and pulling her toward him. He kissed her, his tongue stroking her lips, and she made a soft moan and parted her mouth. He sucked on her lower lip before pulling away.

"One drink, butterfly. Nothing more," he whispered persuasively.

"I – "

"Say yes," he whispered again before kissing the tip of her nose. "You know you're dying to see the inside of my house."

She wouldn't admit it, but she really was. The outside with its wide porch and lush flowerbeds was so completely different from what she had pictured that she was intensely curious about the inside.

"Just one drink, okay?" She licked her lips nervously.

"Yes." He smiled happily as she got out of the car and followed him up the sidewalk to his house.

Once inside she slipped off her heels as he hung her jacket in the closet. She followed him down the hallway and into the kitchen, blinking in surprise when he turned the light on. She had expected something modern and sleek and, while it was modern, she was totally unprepared for the touches of vintage charm.

She ran her hand over the small wooden table and the intricate design carved into the side of it. Four chairs with a matching design surrounded it and the table was sanded and polished to perfection. "This is gorgeous. Where did you buy it?"

"I made it." He pulled a bottle of scotch and two glasses from an upper cabinet.

"What?" Her eyes widened. "You made this table?"

"I did. I like to make furniture. It's a hobby."

"Jax, this – this could be more than a hobby," she said. "The design alone is incredible."

He shrugged as he poured the scotch. "It really is just a hobby."

"What else have you made?"

"Follow me, I'll show you."

He handed her the glass and she followed him out of the kitchen and into the small living room. He pointed to the rocking chair by the fireplace and the small buffet against the far wall. "I made both of those as well."

"They're beautiful. You really should consider trying to sell some of your stuff."

"Nah, it's not that good."

"It is," she insisted. "You have no idea."

He just shrugged again and sat down in the armchair as she studied the rest of the room. One wall had built-in bookshelves that were filled to the brim with books. "You like to read, huh?"

"Yes. Does that surprise you?"

"No," she said. She studied the mantle over the fireplace. "Did you make this as well?"

"Yes. The house was a fixer-upper when I bought it. I've done most of the work myself."

"It's really beautiful."

"Thank you. Drink up." He held his glass of scotch up and she tipped her glass toward him before taking a cautious sip of the liquid.

She rarely drank and she absolutely did not want to get drunk around Jax Anderson. She'd be in his bed with her legs spread wide and screaming his name if she did. The mental image made her shiver with delight and she took another hasty sip before setting the glass on the hearth.

"May I use your bathroom?"

"Upstairs, second door on the left."

"Thanks."

She climbed the staircase and turned down the hall. Had he said the first or second door? She couldn't remember, probably because she was too busy picturing herself naked in his bed. She opened the first door, a thin thread of light was shining out from under it, and peered into the room. Her mouth dropped open.

"You have got to be kidding me," she whispered.

The two bunnies stared at her from the overstuffed armchair they were sitting on. She stepped into the room and stared around in amazement. The floor was tile but a large plush rug covered the middle of it. There were small dog beds scattered around the room, as well as a number of hard plastic baby toys. A large litter box filled to the brim with fresh hay was pushed against one wall and wicker baskets, most of them with large pieces chewed from their edges, were placed strategically around the room.

One of the bunnies hopped down from the armchair and hopped nimbly to the hay bin. It jumped in and began to nibble as the second one stretched and yawned before hopping down and joining it.

"Bunnies?" She whispered. "He has bunnies?"

"What are you doing in here?"

She whipped around at the sound of Jax's voice. He was standing in the doorway and she smiled apologetically. "I'm sorry, I couldn't remember what door you said so I just tried this one."

"It's the next door," he said. "Here, I'll show you."

"Hang on a minute, I want to know why you have bunnies."

Colour stained his cheeks. "They're my pets."

She studied him for so long that his flush deepened. "What?"

"That's seriously adorable."

"Yeah, didn't you say you had to use the bathroom?"

"In a minute," she said. "What are their names?"

He sighed and finished the last of his scotch. "Ricky and Lucy."

She grinned. "That is also adorable."

"Okay, you've seen them. Let's go."

"Can I pet them?"

"Mel, I – "

"Pretty please?" She asked.

He sighed again. "Fine."

"So do you have to like catch them with a net or something?"

"A net?" He rolled his eyes.

"What? I've never had a pet bunny before. Although I have had rabbit stew."

"Not funny." He glowered at her and she giggled.

"I'm sorry."

He squatted down and she watched in amazement as the two bunnies hopped rapidly across the room to him. They flattened their chins on the floor and he rubbed and stroked the tops of their heads and pulled lightly on their long ears before picking up the bigger of the two.

"This is Lucy."

Mel stroked the large white rabbit's ears tentatively before running her fingers along her back. "She's so soft."

"She has some rex in her. That makes her a bit softer."

"Rex?" She asked curiously.

"It's a breed of rabbit."

"How old are they?"

"They're both four years old. I adopted them from a bunny rescue on the outskirts of the city a couple of years ago."

She stepped back as he gently set Lucy on the ground. She hopped back to the hay bin, the smaller grey bunny followed her immediately, and Jax smiled faintly.

"Ricky does whatever Lucy wants."

"Smart bunny." She grinned at him as he brushed the white fur from his suit jacket.

"Since you're up here, I might as well give you a tour of the upstairs."

"Sure," she said, "just give me a minute."

He nodded and she left the room and entered the washroom. She peed quickly and stared at herself in the mirror as she washed her hands. "Get a quick tour and then head home, Thomas. Don't let the fact that he has pet bunnies make you start thinking he's all sweetness and light."

Pep talk over, she let the bathroom and followed Jax down the hall. "This is the guest room. It still needs some work."

"It's nice," she said. It was nice, just lacked the small touches of warmth that permeated the rest of the home.

He led her to the next door. "This is my bedroom."

She stepped into the room. It was decorated in shades of blue and grey and she stared for a long moment at the bed before swallowing and examining the rest of the room.

"Do you like it?"

He was standing behind her, his breath stirring her hair, and she nodded. "It's gorgeous."

"Thank you." His arm snaked around her waist and his hard hand cupped her hip as he brushed her hair aside and kissed the side of her neck. She shuddered against him.

"Jax, you – you said just a drink."

"I lied," he whispered before licking the column of her throat.

"This is such a bad idea," she moaned as his hand moved upward to cup her breast.

"Is it? I think it's an excellent idea." He squeezed her breast firmly, rubbing his thumb across her nipple. "Stay the night with me, butterfly. Let's finish what we started earlier."

"Just tonight, right?" She whispered.

"Yes."

"You can't tell Cal."

"I won't. I promise."

He turned her and pressed a soft kiss against her mouth. "Stay the night, butterfly."

She stared up at him, her entire body vibrating with need for him, and nodded. "Yes."

Chapter 8

Jax gave her a sexy little grin before sliding his hands down and squeezing her ass. "It's going to be so good, butterfly."

"You keep saying that," she said a bit breathlessly. "Maybe it's time you stopped talking and started showing."

"Is that a challenge?"

"Maybe."

"Challenge accepted." His fingers found the zipper on her dress and pulled. He tugged on the material and she shimmied out of it. He bent and picked it up and she watched with amusement as he shook it out and draped it carefully over the dresser.

"What?" He asked.

"For someone who keeps saying he's dying to fuck me, you're certainly taking your sweet time."

He laughed and pulled her into his embrace, his hands reaching for the clasp of her bra. "Are you always this impatient?"

"I just know what I want."

"What is it that you want?"

"You. Inside of me."

"Jesus, butterfly." His pelvis pressed against her and she rubbed herself against his erection before pressing kisses against his throat.

"I suppose you want me to be sweet and submissive?" She asked as she undid his pants and wiggled her hand into his briefs. She wrapped her fingers around his cock and stroked firmly.

"Butterfly, you can be whatever you want to be," he groaned as his pelvis arched.

"Good," she murmured as she tugged his pants and his briefs down before sinking to her knees in front of him.

Without hesitating she slid her mouth over his cock. He made a muttered curse and his hands threaded through her hair to hold her head tightly as she sucked on the head of his cock. He moaned and she took more of him into her mouth, running her tongue over the smooth skin as he twitched and shuddered.

She sucked hard, her cheeks hollowing with the effort, as he pumped his hips back and forth. She gripped the base of him with her hand and stroked him firmly as her tongue teased and tasted the head of his cock.

"Fuck, Mel!" He pushed her back and yanked her to her feet before reaching again for the clasp of her bra. He snapped it open and pulled it from her body, dropping it carelessly to the floor.

"Hey," she teased, "aren't you going to pick that up?"

He didn't reply. He was staring at her breasts with a feral look of hunger and her pelvis throbbed in response.

"Jax?" She whispered.

"Playtime's over, butterfly," he growled.

He stripped off the rest of his clothes and she squealed softly when he picked her up and carried her to the bed. Every muscle in his body was hard as granite and she swallowed nervously as he dropped her on to the bed and covered her body with his. He pushed one hard thigh between her legs and pressed it against her aching pussy.

"Jax, are you okay?"

He bent his head and nipped her neck. "I'm going to eat your sweet pussy until you're screaming my name, butterfly."

She dragged in a harsh breath of air as her pulse thudded heavily. He pressed his lips against it before dipping his head and closing his lips around one nipple. It hardened in his mouth and he growled his satisfaction before sucking firmly. Her back arched and she muttered a soft plea as he kissed the hollow between her breasts and traced his tongue along the soft underside of her breast before taking her other nipple into his mouth. He worried it into the same aching hardness as she rubbed herself shamelessly against his hard thigh.

He slid down her body, kissing and tasting her soft skin before circling her navel with his tongue. He pulled lightly on the waistband of her panties.

"Lift your hips," he growled.

She obeyed immediately and he pulled her panties down her legs with infinite slowness. He kissed her calf before dropping her panties on the floor and moving to his knees beside the bed. His hands circled her waist and he dragged her toward him until her ass was on the edge of the bed and her legs dangled off the side of it.

"Spread your legs," he demanded.

She parted her legs eagerly and he growled softly when her sex was exposed to him.

"Such a pretty little pussy," he whispered.

He pressed a kiss against the small triangle of hair at the top of her sex before licking a slow path down the bare lips of her pussy. She moaned loudly and arched her hips as her hands tugged restlessly at his hair.

"Jax, please."

"Patience, butterfly." He took her hands, his fingers closing around her wrists, and held them tightly at her sides. Trapped, she could only writhe against him helplessly as he pressed his tongue between her wet lips and licked at her clit. He stroked it repeatedly, each brush bringing her closer and closer to the edge, and she made a loud whimper of need.

He sucked firmly on her clit and she clamped her thighs around his head as her back arched and she cried out. He released her wrists and pried her legs apart, holding them firmly in his big hands before sucking on her clit again.

She grabbed the bedcover in her hands, clenching it tightly, and twisting and turning against Jax's warm mouth. He rubbed his tongue over her clit and her entire body lifted from the bed as she screamed his name and came violently against his mouth. He held her firmly as she shuddered and moaned before collapsing against the bed.

She breathed harshly, dragging oxygen in and out of her lungs, as Jax stood and opened the drawer of the bedside table. He pulled out a condom and tore open the foil package, rolling it on hurriedly before kneeling between her splayed thighs.

"Open your eyes, butterfly," he said.

Her eyelids fluttered open as he propped himself above her and kissed her. She could taste herself on his lips and it sent another shiver of desire through her.

"Jax, I want you to fuck me," she moaned as he rubbed the head of his cock against her clit.

"Then put me inside of you, butterfly," he whispered into her ear before sucking lightly on her earlobe.

She reached eagerly between their bodies and grasped his cock, guiding it toward her wet entrance. He moaned when the head of his cock slipped inside of her and she bit her bottom lip.

"You're so damn big," she muttered.

He grinned at her as he pushed his way steadily into her wet and willing body. "You're so damn tight."

He seated himself fully in her, both of them gasping with pleasure when he began a slow slide and retreat motion. Almost immediately he began to move faster and she wrapped her legs around his lean hips and urged him on.

"Fuck, butterfly," he muttered, "I'm about to embarrass myself."

She grinned at him before nipping at his thick neck and then using her tongue to trace the tattoo that covered it. "I won't hold it against you."

"Touch yourself," he demanded.

She squeezed her hand between their bodies and rubbed lightly at her swollen clit. It was still sensitive and she squeezed her inner muscles around Jax's cock at the feel of her fingers. He groaned loudly and jerked against her.

"Shit, bad idea." He stared at her. "Stop that, butterfly."

She shook her head and licked his collarbone. "No way. It feels so good, Jax."

She rubbed again at her clit as Jax slid in and out of her and squeezed him once more.

"I'm going to fucking come if you keep doing that, Melanie," he grunted.

"Self-control is very important, Jax."

"Mel, please," he suddenly begged and the need in his deep voice brought on a powerful wave of lust deep inside of her.

She rubbed furiously at her clit as he thrust almost desperately in and out of her.

"You feel so good, Jax," she panted into his ear. She wanted to make him lose control. She wanted to watch his face as he came inside of her and she bit the base of his neck, marking him as hers.

He bent his head and kissed her hard on the mouth, sliding his tongue between her lips just as her orgasm, unexpected and immensely satisfying, started through her. Her pussy squeezed around him as she moaned into his mouth. He broke the kiss, his back arching, and he threw his head back and made a short, hoarse howl of pleasure as he climaxed deep inside of her.

He collapsed against her, breathing harshly, and she stroked his damp back as he kissed the hollow of her throat.

"So good," he murmured into her skin.

"Yes," she panted.

He rolled off of her and disposed of the condom before turning her on her side and spooning her. She was sleepy but she forced her weary eyelids open. She shouldn't stay the night with him. There was no point in –

As if he had read her mind, Jax mumbled, "Stay the night, butterfly."

She hesitated and he pulled her more tightly against him. "Stay."

"Okay," she whispered.

He nuzzled the back of her neck affectionately before cupping her breast possessively. She closed her eyes and drifted to sleep.

* * *

"Jules, you're selling the house?" Mary gave her a look of surprise.

"I'm thinking about it." Julie shifted on the couch as she stared around the room. "I hate everything here."

"Yeah, but, you grew up in this house."

"It doesn't hold any good memories for me."

"I suppose it doesn't," Mary replied. "Oh! You should totally buy a condo downtown. Live in one of those luxury high rises and experience everything the city has to offer."

Julie laughed. "Mary, you know that isn't me,"

"But it could be," Mary said. "You're just starting to discover who you really are. You might make some mistakes along the way but you're richer than hell, you can afford to make mistakes."

"I can't live in a condo downtown, Mary. It isn't my style and it definitely isn't Court's."

"Are you and Court moving in together?" Mary asked.

Julie shrugged. "We haven't talked about it but we spend every night together, either at his place or mine."

"Yeah but, living together is a totally different thing, Jules."

"How's Mark doing?" Julie asked abruptly. "Court said he was out sick for a couple of days."

"He has that bug that's been going around. He's on the mend though."

"You've been dating him for a while now," Julie said.

"He's a good guy."

"So is Court."

Mary leaned forward. "Honey, I know he is. I just think you might be moving a little too fast. I've been dating Mark for the same amount of time you've been dating Court, and you don't see us moving in together or declaring our love."

Julie sighed. "Why is everyone so insistent that Court and I don't love each other?"

"Because knowing someone's sexual likes and dislikes isn't love, Jules," Mary said gently.

"I know more than that about Court," Julie said hotly.

"Do you? What's his favourite colour? Where did he grow up? How is he with money? Does he wants kids?" Mary asked.

Julie glared at her. "I thought you would be happy for me, Mary. Didn't you say I needed to find Mr. Right? Well, I've found him."

"I know you think you have, but, honey, he's your first real boyfriend and he just got out of a bad relationship. Mark told me all about Janine. Court really loved her. He wanted to marry her and less than a year later he's declaring his love for you. I don't want you to be some sort of rebound for him."

"Did Mark also tell you that Janine lied to him and cheated on him? Court and I have talked about Janine and I'm not worried, Mary. Court loves me and I love him and I'm sick to death of people insisting we can't possibly be in love. Frankly, it's none of your business!"

Mary blinked in surprise at her sudden anger before nodding. "You're right, Jules. It isn't any of my business and I apologize."

"Thank you," Julie said as Mary leaned forward and picked up the stack of papers on the coffee table.

"What are these?"

"Court printed them off for me. It's information about the architectural design course."

Mary leafed through them before glancing at Julie. "You'd have to move."

"I know."

"What does Court think of that?"

"He thinks I should do it."

"Really?" Mary said thoughtfully. "That's admirable of him. Not many men in a new relationship would be urging their girlfriend to move away from them."

Julie didn't reply and Mary set the papers on the table. "Honey, do you still want to be an architect?"

"I – I don't know," Julie said honestly. "I thought I did but the idea of moving away from Court makes me sick to my stomach."

"You shouldn't base your life on a guy, Jules," Mary said gently.

"I know that," Julie replied. "But I can't help the way I feel."

"I know. I guess you need to decide if this is the career you want. If it isn't, what do you want?"

"Sometimes I think I just want to be a wife and a mom. Is that awful, Mary? Shouldn't I want a career?"

Mary shook her head. "It isn't awful. Besides, from what my sister says, being a mom is a full time career in itself."

"I really don't know what to do," Julie confessed. "Court is really pushing me to apply for this course and I don't want to disappoint him, you know?"

"I do, but you have to do what's right for you, Jules, not what's right for Court."

"I don't want to disappoint him," Julie repeated. "He has so much faith in me and he's so adamant that I would be good at this. Which, honestly, I don't know if I would be. I mean, how would I even know?"

"I guess you wouldn't unless you tried."

"I guess," Julie said. She stood and smiled at Mary, "C'mon, let's have some lunch and you can tell me all about Mark. I feel like we haven't had girl time in forever."

She left the room and Mary, with a final glance at the papers on the table, followed her.

Chapter 9

"This is an important day, Jax."

When Jax didn't reply, Mr. Golden rapped sharply on his desk. "Jax!"

"Sorry, Mr. Golden." Jax forced himself to pay attention as Jimmy frowned deeply. Christ, he needed to get it together. It had been nearly a week since he had seen Mel and his obsession with her was growing. He had thought that spending the night with her would have ended his obsession but fuck, he had never been more wrong about anything in his life. He supposed he should count himself lucky that he didn't have her cell number or he'd be texting her like a lovesick puppy and begging for another round in the sack.

"Jax!"

He shook his head to clear it and gazed into Jimmy Golden's disgruntled face. "Sorry, sir."

"What is going on with you?" Jimmy asked.

"Nothing, sir."

"Then get your head out of the clouds and back in the game."

"Yes, sir."

Jimmy tapped one finger on his desk. "I'm promoting you to lieutenant."

Jax's eyes widened and he stared in disbelief at Jimmy. The older man nodded.

"I'm not kidding."

"Thank you, Mr. Golden."

"You're welcome. Hell, I should have promoted you the minute that fucker Chan sent me Johnson's goddamn head in that cooler but I – well, you're like a son to me, Jax, and I didn't want you to end up the same way."

Jax felt a small trickle of guilt run down his spine. He shook it off immediately. Now was not the time to start thinking that Golden was a nice guy. He might have saved his life as a teenager but Jax had paid that debt repeatedly. He didn't owe Golden anything."

Jimmy suddenly laughed. "You could kill a man with your bare hands and I'm worried that Chan will get to you."

"I won't let you down, sir," Jax said solemnly.

"I know you won't, son," Jimmy replied. "I'm meeting with Mulroney tomorrow at two. I want you to be there."

"Yes, sir." He sat a moment longer as Jimmy studied the computer screen in front of him.

Jimmy glanced up and with an impatient wave, said, "You're dismissed, Jax."

"Thank you, sir."

He left Jimmy's office and headed into the club. He sat at the bar, nodding his thanks when the bartender, Rachel, set a whiskey in front of him, and sipped at it. He needed to inform Darvin that he'd been promoted. As soon as he was told the shipment drop location, he'd pass the information along and he'd finally be free of the controlling bastard.

He took another sip of whiskey, barely feeling the burn in his throat, before staring moodily at the top of the bar. If he was lucky in another month he'd be doing exactly what the FBI agent had promised – lying on a warm beach where no one had ever heard of Jax Anderson or Jimmy Golden.

What about Mel?

He shoved that voice out of his head. What about her? They had slept together once and neither of them wanted anything more.

Are you sure about that?

Positive. He didn't date. Giving Jimmy Golden any type of leverage over you was a very bad idea, he had seen it numerous times over the years. Mulroney's wife was missing the pinkie on her right hand because Mulroney had fucked up. He had decided years ago that he wouldn't give Golden that type of power over him and he'd never wavered from that.

Sleeping with her one more time wouldn't be dangerous, his mind whispered persuasively. *Golden would never suspect that you and a woman like Melanie Thomas would ever be sleeping together. She's about as far from your type as you can get.*

That was very true but the thought of Golden hurting Mel made his stomach twist and, for the first time in years, a trickle of fear slithered down his spine. He wouldn't let Mel be tormented or used as some kind of pawn by Golden. The best thing to do was to stay as far away from Melanie Thomas as he possibly could.

"Jesus, Jax, who died?"

Cal sat down next to him, adjusting his tie, before clapping Jax on the back.

"Hey, Cal." Jax swallowed the last of his whiskey and put his hand over the glass when Rachel appeared with a bottle. She gave him a slow and seductive smile and he stared evenly at her until she flushed and moved away. The woman had been trying to seduce him since she started three months ago but he had no interest in her. She hadn't yet realized what a bad idea it was to sleep with anyone in Golden's employment.

"You tapping that?" Cal asked.

Jax shook his head and Cal grinned at him. "Why not? She's looking at you like you're a piece of candy."

"She's not my type and she works for Golden. I don't mix business with pleasure."

"Fair enough," Cal said. "I, on the other hand, don't have a problem with it."

He winked at Rachel, who had moved to the far end of the bar, and she rolled her eyes before turning her back to them.

"I feel like Rachel may not be receptive to your charm, Calvin," Jax said.

"Not yet but I'll win her over," Cal said. "Seriously though, is everything okay? You looked like you were about a million miles away when I sat down."

For one brief moment, Jax pictured himself telling Cal that he was obsessed with his sister. That he had taken her to his bed and now couldn't stop thinking about her. He dismissed the ridiculous idea immediately. Mel had specifically asked him not to tell Cal and he wouldn't disappoint her. Besides, Cal was a good guy but if he was in his place, he sure as hell wouldn't want to hear some guy talking about fucking his baby sister.

Jimmy had asked him to win Cal's trust, to become friends with him, and the ironic thing was he actually did like Cal. They had gone to a baseball game two nights ago and he had been surprised at how much he enjoyed it. Cal was a talker and Jax had subtly encouraged the family stories. It was pathetic but he wanted to know more about Melanie.

He sighed inwardly. Cal was smart and funny and totally wasting his potential working for Jimmy. Another twinge of guilt went through him. He wondered briefly if Cal would go back to working for the escort agency when Jimmy's drug empire finally caved in. Hell, there were more than a few innocent people who worked in the night club and Jimmy's chain of restaurants who would suffer when their boss was arrested.

You can't think about that. Golden needs to be stopped and you know that.

Yeah, he did.

"Jax?"

"Just tired," he said abruptly.

Cal studied him carefully for a moment before slapping him on the back. "Mom wants me to invite you to the family barbeque this weekend."

"What?"

"Family. Barbeque. Last one of the summer." Cal grinned at him. "It's a tradition."

"If it's a family barbeque then I shouldn't go," Jax said.

"Nah, it's not like that. My mom is forever inviting poor little orphan waifs like yourself to our family functions."

"Orphan waif?"

Cal shrugged. "I know you don't have any family. Hell, from what I've heard around the club you don't have that many friends either."

"I like my space," Jax grunted.

"If you don't come to the barbeque, you'll never get a nickname from my mom. Is that what you want, Jax? Is it?" Cal asked dramatically.

Jax bit back his smile. He couldn't go to the barbeque. Melanie would be there and he needed to stay away from her. It didn't matter if all he could think about was her soft voice and warm body or the way she had looked when she was coming. He had asked her for one night and gotten it. He needed to forget her.

"Well?" Cal asked? "Are you coming or not?"

"Sure."

Asshole!

"Great!" Cal slapped him on the back before standing and buttoning his jacket. "It's on Sunday. Dinner starts around five but you can show up any time after three. Okay?"

"Should I bring anything?"

"Nah. Mom will have enough food to feed an army. Are you sticking around tonight?"

Jax shook his head. "No, Mr. Golden is hosting a dinner party at his place. I'll be at that for a few hours and then heading home."

"Count yourself lucky," Cal said. "Apparently we have some 'B-list' movie star coming in tonight and he's invited about thirty of his closest friends. It's going to be a fucking zoo in here."

As Cal walked away, Jax rubbed wearily at his forehead. He shouldn't have said he would go to the damn barbeque but the thought of seeing Mel again was too tempting to resist. Besides, it's not like they were going to have sex in the bathroom again. In a few weeks' time Jax Anderson would be gone and he'd never see her again. There was no harm in going to the barbeque just to see her, to smell her sweet scent, one last time.

* * *

Jax studied the produce in front of him before selecting a fresh bunch of carrots, their green tops damp, and placing it in the shopping basket slung over his arm. It was a twenty-four-hour grocery store but at two in the morning, there was only one other person roaming the produce aisle. The old man shuffled out of produce and toward the dairy section, his cane making a rhythmic thumping on the worn linoleum, as a third man appeared.

He carried a shopping basket as well and he placed potatoes and a head of cauliflower in it as he moved toward Jax. He picked up a green pepper, testing the weight of it in his hand, and without looking at Jax, said, "What's the news?"

"I'm in. He promoted me earlier today."

Agent Darvin placed the green pepper in his basket and picked up an eggplant. "That's very good news. When's the next deal?"

"I don't know yet. I'll let you know," Jax replied.

"Good."

Keeping his eyes on the spinach in front of him, Jax said, "As soon as I tell you, I want out."

"We can't do that. Not yet."

"Bullshit. I told you I'd find out where he was delivering drugs and you said you'd give me a new life."

"And we will. But unless Golden's there himself, we can't bust him. We need him personally delivering it and we need you to help make that happen."

"It's never going to happen. I told you - he's not stupid," Jax said.

"If he was left with no choice, he would," the agent said.

"What do you mean?"

"I mean, you find out where the next drug deal is and let us worry about the rest."

"Just how the hell are you going to do that?"

"Like I said - don't worry about it. Just find out the information we need."

With a soft snort of disgust, Jax walked away.

* * *

"Butterfly, you're short a place setting," Darla said.

Mel frowned at the picnic table and mentally counted in her head. "I'm not, Mom."

"You are. I told Cal to bring Jax with him."

"You what?" Mel glanced down at herself as Julie set out the wineglasses.

"I told Cal to bring Jax with him," Darla repeated.

"Why would you do that?" Mel rubbed frantically at the stain on the front of her sundress. She groaned inwardly as she remembered the state of her hair. She hadn't done anything with it this morning, just threw her damp hair into a bun on the top of her head, and she wasn't wearing a lick of makeup.

"Because I know you like him, butterfly," Darla said cheerfully.

Mel gaped at her mother before staring accusingly at Julie. Julie shook her head. "I didn't say anything, Mel, I swear."

"Oh please, I'm your mother," Darla snorted. "Do you really think I need someone else to tell me when my girl likes a boy?"

"I don't like Jax Anderson, mom," Mel lied hotly.

"No?" Darla said cheerfully. "Well then what do you care if he comes to the barbeque today?"

"I don't," Mel said. "Excuse me."

She hurried toward the patio doors and shut it behind her before bolting up the stairs to the bathroom. It was locked and she rattled the doorknob as Court yelled, "Occupied!"

"I know you're playing Candy Crush in there, Court!" She snapped.

"Am not. I just can't be rushed when I'm peeing," he said conversationally. "Use the one downstairs."

She rolled her eyes and marched down the hall to her old bedroom. Her parents had converted it into a guest room, but her old bed was still there as well as her vanity, and she bent and checked her reflection in the mirror.

"Dammit," she sighed. Her cheeks were flushed, her hair was a rat's nest on top of her head and she had a zit starting on her chin.

"I'm going to kill my mother," she muttered to herself as she poked at the zit.

"Matricide doesn't seem to be your thing, butterfly."

She whipped around, staring wide-eyed at Jax Anderson. He was standing in the doorway and he let his gaze drop down her body as a slow grin crossed his face.

Mel's pulse was starting to pound and she licked her lips as she looked him over. He was wearing a tight-fitting green t-shirt with faded and worn jeans and he looked positively delicious. A vision of being under him, of tracing her fingers across his abs, brought a surge of wetness to her panties and she inhaled sharply. Fuck, she wanted him badly.

She had thought she was done with him after their night together. She had left early the next morning, he hadn't asked her to stay, and she had spent the last week doing her best to forget exactly how it felt to be in Jax Anderson's bed. She thought she'd done a good job of it. It wasn't like she had thought of him the entire week, maybe only half of it.

She took a deep breath and smoothed her sundress nervously before starting toward him. She would say hello and not act like she wanted to fuck him senseless. She would have some goddamn self-control.

Jax watched as Mel took a deep breath and smoothed her dress. She looked amazing – her hair was piled on top of her head and her face was free of makeup. He could smell her perfume and he reached out and touched her arm as she walked by him.

"Hello, butterfly. Have you missed me?"

He ached to wrap his hand around her arm, push her up against the wall and bury himself deep inside of her. The smell of her perfume was all around him and he swallowed heavily as she turned to face him.

She had the strangest look on her face, desire and anxiety warring across it, and he made a muffled noise of surprise when her own hand clutched his arm and she yanked him into the room. She slammed the door shut and locked it before pushing him up against the wall.

"Mel, what's – "

She pressed her body against him and stood on her tiptoes before kissing him with desperate need. He groaned and slid his arms around her waist, locking his hands together in the small of her back as he returned her kiss. She was shoving her hand down his pants and he gasped harshly when her fingers closed around him and she stroked him urgently.

"Christ, butterfly. That's quite the hello," he muttered.

"Shut up," she whispered. "I want you, Jax."

He grinned at her and turned her around before pushing her up against the wall. She unzipped his jeans as he yanked a condom from his pocket and tore at the foil.

"Do you always carry a condom in your pocket," she panted into his ear as she pushed his jeans and his briefs down to his knees.

"I figured I should have one just in case we ran into each other in the bathroom," he said.

"Presumptuous," she said as he rolled the condom onto his cock.

"Says the girl who's attacking me in the guest room."

He pushed her sundress up to her waist and pulled her panties down her legs. She kicked them off impatiently as he lifted her up.

"Well, if you're not interested, we can stop right now," she said breathlessly as she wrapped her legs around his hips.

"Like you want to stop." He kissed the tip of her nose. "Fucking me again is all you've thought about for the last week. Admit it."

"I've barely thought of you at all, Mr. Anderson. I don't know what – "

She made a loud cry of need as Jax shifted her slightly and his cock slipped along her swollen and sensitive clit. He probed at her tight entrance and she made another harsh cry of longing.

"Quiet, butterfly," he muttered.

She ignored him as she arched her pelvis against his. She needed him inside of her, her desire had become a living, pulsing thing, and if she didn't have him soon she would go mad.

"Jax, now!" She said loudly and he clamped his hand over her mouth before entering her with one hard thrust.

She cried out against his hand, her fingers clutching at his shoulders as he thrust back and forth. The picture beside her rattled on the wall before giving up its tenuous cling to the nail and falling. Jax released her mouth and caught it with one hand, even through her haze of pleasure she was astounded by his reflexes, and set it on the vanity beside them.

She squeezed him tightly as he lifted her a little higher, his hands clamping down on her hips, before thrusting in and out of her.

"Oh fuck, oh fuck," she muttered harshly, "it feels so good, Jax."

He buried his face in her neck, nipping at her soft skin, as she squeezed her legs around his hips and urged him on with soft cries and moans.

"Harder, Jax, please," she begged into his ear.

He kissed her again, their tongues darting in and out of each other's mouths as he drove in and out of her. She wiggled one hand between them, biting down on his bottom lip when she ran her trembling fingers over her clit.

"I'm going to come," she moaned against his mouth.

"Yes," he groaned. "Now, Mel."

She brushed the tips of her fingers over her clit twice more as Jax surged in and out of her. Her orgasm flooded through her, setting her nerve endings on fire as she shook and twitched and stuffed her face into his broad neck to muffle her cries of ecstasy.

"Fuck!" He muttered as he pinned her against the wall. His entire body shook, his hands dug painfully into her hips and he swore again as he thrust wildly in and out. She clung tightly to him as he came, running her hands over the soft material of his t-shirt as he shuddered against her.

They rested for a moment, both of them breathing harshly, before he eased out of her. He took of the condom, tying the end of it, as she tugged on her panties and reached for a tissue from the box on the vanity.

"Give it to me," she said.

He dropped it into the tissue and she buried it deep in the small trash bin as he pulled his jeans up over his hips. She straightened her dress and smiled nervously at him when he pulled her back into his arms and kissed her lightly.

"Hello, butterfly."

"Hi, Jax."

"This is turning out to be the best barbeque ever," he said and she blushed furiously.

"I'm sorry, that was totally inappropriate of me," she said.

"Hey, I get it. I'm irresistible," he replied as he reached down and squeezed her ass.

She rolled her eyes and he grinned. "I take it you missed me this week?"

"No, just really horny today," she said.

"Cruel." He kissed her throat and she shivered as a new wave of excitement swept through her. "I missed you, butterfly."

"You did?" She whispered.

"Yes. All I could think about was how good you looked naked and in my bed." He sucked on her earlobe and palmed her breast, running his thumb over her tight nipple.

"We really have to stop having sex at my parents' house," she said.

"You're right," he said seriously.

Disappointment flooded through her and she tried to step away from him. He tightened his hold on her before dipping his head and licking her mouth. "That's why you should give me your address, butterfly. I'll come by after the barbeque."

"I thought you didn't date."

"This isn't dating. This is fucking," he said.

She swallowed down the odd lump that rose in her throat. "One night of fucking, that's what you said, Jax."

"Yet here we are," he nuzzled her neck and slid his hand under sundress before cupping her pussy through her damp panties. "One more night, butterfly. There's still so much more I want to do to you."

"Just one more night," she gasped as he rubbed her clit through her panties.

"That's right," he agreed.

She licked her lips nervously as he stroked her lightly through her panties. "Okay," she finally whispered. "Just one more night and then – "

There was a light knock on the door and Julie's soft voice drifted through it, "Mel? Cal's looking for Jax. He'll be up here any minute."

"Shit," she muttered.

Jax grinned at her and kissed her lightly. "Text me your address, Mel."

He unlocked the door and opened it, smiling at Julie. "Hello, Julie."

"Um, hi, Mr. Anderson. How are you?"

"Call me Jax, won't you?"

"Um, sure." Julie took a nervous step backward as Jax winked at Mel before striding down the hallway and down the stairs.

"Jax, where were you?" Cal's voice floated up the stairs as Mel grabbed Julie's hand and nearly yanked her into the small room. She shut the door and stared wide-eyed at Julie.

"I did it again."

"Oops?" Julie said with a small grin.

"Not funny, Jules!" Mel paced back and forth. "It was supposed to be one night, just one night of sweaty, mind-blowing sex, and nothing more! That's what we agreed to. I went home with him last weekend and we had sex all night and that was supposed to be it."

Julie didn't reply and Mel smacked herself in the forehead with the heel of her palm. "I take one look at him and lose my goddamn mind. I practically attacked him."

"He didn't seem to mind," Julie said.

Mel stopped pacing and stared at her. "How did you know we were in here?"

"I was upstairs using the bathroom and um, heard you," Julie said.

"Oh my God," Mel groaned. "What if it had been Cal who heard us? From what I can tell, he and Jax are becoming friends."

"He didn't," Julie said soothingly. "I went back downstairs and heard Cal asking where Jax was so I ran up here to warn you."

Mel grabbed Julie's hand. "Thank you. Seriously, thank you."

"You're welcome."

"What am I doing, Jules?" Mel sighed.

"Dating a bad boy?" She suggested.

"He doesn't want to date. He just wants sex," Mel replied.

"Is that what you want?"

"I don't know. It makes sense not to date. We have nothing in common."

"How do you know that for sure?" Julie asked. "Maybe you have more in common than you think."

"I doubt that," Mel replied. "He wants to come over to my place after the barbeque and dammit, if I'm not going to let him. Am I making a mistake, Jules?"

"I don't think so. At least, not if both of you are fine with just, you know, sleeping together," Julie said hesitantly.

"Right." Mel tugged at the bottom of her dress. "How do I look?"

"Your throat is a little red," Julie said.

"Shit." She touched the spot where Jax had nipped her. "How noticeable is it?"

"Not that noticeable," Julie reassured her.

"Thanks." Mel hesitated before giving her a tight hug. "Court's a lucky guy, Julie."

Julie smiled. "I'm lucky to have him. Now, we'd better get back downstairs before they start to wonder where we are."

Chapter 10

She opened the door of her apartment, her heart starting up a crazy jumbled beat, and smiled uncertainly at him. He leaned against the door frame and returned her smile with a lazy heat that made her tremble with anticipation.

"Hi," she said.

"Hello, butterfly."

A ribbon of heat twisted through her. God, it did things to her to hear him say her childhood nickname in his raspy voice.

"Come in."

She hung his coat in the closet as he took off his shoes. He followed her down the hallway and into the kitchen.

"Did you come straight here from the barbeque?"

She had practically flown home, showering quickly and applying some makeup before slipping into her favourite pair of jeans and a tank top.

He shook his head. "I stopped at home to feed Ricky and Lucy."

A smile crossed her face and he tugged lightly on a lock of her dark hair. "What?"

She shrugged. "You just don't seem like the pet bunny type."

"There's a lot you don't know about me, butterfly," he said teasingly.

She studied him carefully. "Yes, I guess there is."

An odd current of tension shimmered between them and she cleared her throat nervously. "Are you hungry? I could make us something to eat."

He shook his head. "God, no. I ate way too much at the barbeque. There's no delicate way to tell you this but your mother is a food pusher."

She laughed and the slight tension was broken. "She really is. I'm surprised I don't weigh three hundred pounds."

His gaze dropped to her body and she licked her lips as her pulse sped up. "Would you like to uh…"

She trailed off. How did one just go about asking a man to join her in the bedroom for sex without sounding like a total whore?

"How about a tour?" He suggested.

"Good idea," she said with a smile of relief. She led him from the kitchen, jumping a bit when his hand curled around hers.

"Relax, butterfly," he said softly.

"Right," she cleared her throat again before showing him the living room. "This is the living room."

"It's nice," he said as he stood behind her. He pushed her hair to the side and dropped a warm kiss on the back of her neck. She shuddered and leaned against him as he put his arms around her and rubbed her flat belly.

"I like your artwork." He kissed her neck again as he studied the painting over the fireplace.

"Thanks. I painted it."

His hands, which had begun to unbutton her jeans, stilled and he moved away from her to study the painting more closely. "Really?"

"Yes. Both Court and I love art. We've taken a few art classes over the years."

"It's amazing."

She laughed. "You're being generous."

"I'm not."

"You are," she said before holding out her hand. "Come on, I'll show you the rest."

He followed her down the hallway as she pointed out the guest bathroom and the spare bedroom. It had a small twin bed and an easel was set up in the one corner.

"This is where you paint?"

She nodded. "Mostly. Sometimes I paint in the living room while I'm watching TV."

"Can I see your latest?"

She shook her head. "I don't really like to show people a canvas until it's done."

"Okay." He kissed her knuckles and she tugged him out of the bedroom and shut the door firmly behind her.

"This is my bedroom." She opened the door and he followed her into the room.

"It's nice."

"It's not as big as yours," she said. "And the bed is only a double, not a king."

"There are advantages to a small bed," he whispered before drawing her into his embrace. "Don't you think?"

She nodded and moaned when he traced her collarbone with the tip of one rough finger. "You know," he said suddenly, "I think your mother is on to us."

"She thinks I like you," Mel said.

"And do you?"

She hesitated before nodding. "Yes, I do."

He leaned in and cupped her face before rubbing his thumb across her cheekbone. "I like you too, butterfly."

He pressed a light kiss against her mouth, pulling back when she parted her lips. "In fact, I'm afraid I might be a little obsessed with you."

She stared up at him. She was struck with the sudden urge to tell him she wanted more. To say fuck their differences and find out if their desire for each other could be something more. She closed her eyes and silently berated herself as he kissed a soft path down her throat. Jax had made it perfectly clear what he wanted and she wouldn't try to change his mind. Besides, she could understand his obsession. He had become some kind of obsession for her as well and she hoped that one more night would end their mutual obsession.

Keep telling yourself that, Thomas. Maybe it'll make it true.

"Mel?"

She opened her eyes. Jax was giving her a look of concern and he threaded his hand through her hair. "Do you still want to do this?"

"Hell, yes," she said.

"Good."

He kissed her deeply and she inhaled his already-familiar scent as he tugged her tank top over her head and unhooked her bra. He cupped her breasts almost reverently and coaxed her nipples into an aching hardness.

He pressed a soft kiss in the hollow between her breasts. "You are the most beautiful woman I have ever met, butterfly."

She stared at him. She had no sense that he was just trying to flatter her and warmth spread through her as she reached out and traced the scar on his face. "Thank you. You're beautiful too."

He smiled and pressed a light kiss on the tip of one throbbing nipple. She arched her back, her hands sliding into his hair and he smiled again before rubbing his rough cheek against her soft skin.

"You're wearing entirely too many clothes."

"So are you." She pulled impatiently at his t-shirt and he stripped out of it before draping it neatly on top of her dresser. She studied his hard body in the dim light.

"Your body is amazing. You know that, right?"

He actually blushed a little and she laughed before unbuttoning his jeans. "Also, you're kind of adorable when you blush."

He pulled her forward and reached for the button on her jeans. "I do not blush, Ms. Thomas."

Quickly, they helped each other out of their clothes and she teased him gently again when he picked up their clothes from the floor and placed them neatly on the dresser.

"So beautiful," Jax murmured when she was standing naked in front of him. "I can't get enough of you, butterfly."

She pushed him on to his back on the bed and straddled his hips before letting her fingers drift back and forth over his hard chest. "God, your body is like granite. How often do you work out?"

"Just about every day," he replied.

She shook her head. "I could never have that kind of dedication when it comes to exercise. Although, maybe I should try."

"No, don't. Your body is perfection," he said immediately before squeezing her hips.

She leaned over him and brushed her breasts against his chest, enjoying his sharp inhale. "This is madness. You know that right?"

"I do," he agreed before cupping her ass and squeezing it lightly. "But I'm enjoying every fucking minute of it."

She nipped at his earlobe. "I am too."

He stroked her back as she rubbed her pussy against his erection, and made a low moan of pleasure. "Fuck, butterfly, you make me so goddamn hot I can't think straight."

"Good," she said before tracing his ear with her tongue. She straightened and he watched as she took out a condom from the nightstand. He slipped his hand between her thighs and rubbed at her clit.

"You're distracting me," she admonished lightly as she tore at the foil wrapper. Her fingers were trembling and she moaned under her breath when he tugged lightly at her clit. With sudden impatience, she ripped the foil open and pulled out the condom before scooting back. She studied his cock, marveling inwardly again at the size of it, and squeezed the base firmly.

He gasped with pleasure, his hips arching against her hand as she stroked and rubbed him until a bead of precum appeared at the top. She leaned down and licked it away, smiling at his groan, and pulled back when his hands threaded through her hair.

"Please, butterfly," he whispered. "Please."

"I like it when you beg," she teased before slowly rolling the condom on to his cock.

She positioned herself above him, his hands on her hips steadying her, and guided his cock to her wet entrance. As the head slipped inside of her, they both moaned and she made herself stop. Her legs were trembling and she was aching to take his entire cock but she waited.

His eyes opened and he gave her a look of dark desire that had her pulse racing. "Butterfly, stop teasing."

She smiled and slowly sank down on his cock. She bit at her bottom lip as she stretched around him. He was lying perfectly still beneath her and she took his hands and placed them on her breasts. He kneaded them lightly and she closed her eyes before rocking back and forth. The motion put delicious pleasure against her g-spot and she rocked faster as he watched her take what she wanted from him.

She rocked harder and faster, her hands digging into his chest as he pinched her nipples. The slight pain mixed with the pleasure and she cried out as he pinched her nipples again.

"Jax, oh, oh…"

The tension was building inside of her and with a final cry, she threw her head back and rubbed herself furiously against Jax's cock. Her orgasm roared through her and she shuddered wildly before collapsing against his chest.

He rubbed her back, waiting patiently for her breathing to slow, and then kissed her shoulder. "Turn around, Mel."

She eased off of him and straddled him backwards. He helped her position herself and groaned harshly when she sank on to his cock again. He rubbed her ass as she stared at him over her shoulder. Her legs were still trembling from her orgasm but when he raised his legs, she braced her hands on his knees and rode him with slow and deliberate movements.

"Fuck, just like that," he muttered as his pelvis rose and fell. "You're so goddamn tight."

His hands tightened around her hips and he held her firmly as he pumped in and out. She rubbed her clit lightly, the new pleasure surging within her making her tighten around him. He cursed and thrust harder and faster.

She bounced up and down, her fingers rubbing more firmly and when her orgasm washed over her, sudden and completely unexpected, she arched her back and cried his name. He groaned and thrust furiously until his body stiffened and he came with a hoarse shout. She rested her forehead on his knees as he stroked her back and ass with his warm hands.

"Christ, Mel," he mumbled as she climbed off of him and collapsed on her side next to him.

He rolled to face her and as he cupped her face a small shudder of pleasure went through her.

You're in so much trouble, Thomas.

* * *

"Will you tell me how this happened?"

It was half an hour later. They were lying in the bed together and Jax's hand, which had been tracing lazy circles on her naked back, slowed to a stop as Mel touched the scar on his face.

She waited patiently. She was almost positive he wouldn't tell her but he tugged her a little closer and kissed the top of her head before saying, "I was trying to protect my aunt."

She lifted her head and stared at him. "You got it as a child?"

He nodded. "You're surprised."

"A little. I thought you got it working for Golden."

"No."

She sat up and reached for the glass of water on the nightstand, drinking a few swallows before handing it to him. He finished the water and leaned back against the headboard, staring at his hands, as she stroked his arm lightly.

"What happened?"

"I had only been living with her for a few months and I was naïve and stupid enough to think that she actually cared about me. I hadn't realized just how big of a hold the drugs had on her, you know?"

She nodded and scooted a little closer as he shifted in the bed.

"Her boyfriend – he was also her drug dealer – was over and they got into a fight. He pulled a knife on her and I tried to protect her. He sliced me open."

"Oh my God, Jax." She stared horrified at him and he squeezed her leg lightly.

"There was a lot of blood and it sent both my aunt and her boyfriend into a panic. He left and she took me to the hospital. She made me tell them that I tripped and fell into a window and was cut by the broken glass. She said if I didn't lie about it they would take me away to a foster home where they'd really hurt me."

"I'm so sorry," she whispered.

He shrugged. "It was a long time ago."

"Did you – was there any part of your childhood that was good, Jax?"

A small smile crossed his face. "Mr. Golden threw me a surprise birthday party when I turned fourteen. His daughter, Jade, invited a bunch of my classmates and Mr. Golden rented one of those big bounce-house things, you know? We were way too old for it but it was actually kind of fun. Twelve teen boys jumping in this stupid bouncy house, trying to beat the shit out of each other as we jumped. He rented a giant screen and projector for the backyard and we ate pizza and popcorn and watched all my favourite movies."

"It sounds nice," she said.

"It was," he replied.

"You love him, don't you?"

He frowned at her. "Who?"

"Golden."

A hard look came over his face and he shook his head. "No, I don't."

She stared puzzled at him as he turned away from her. She cupped his face and made him look at her. "Jax, what's wrong?"

"Nothing."

"There is. Don't shut me out," she said.

He sighed. "I don't love him, Mel. I owe him and he saved my life but he isn't a good man."

"Because he's a drug dealer?"

He pulled his face free of her hand and looked away again. "No."

She was silent for a moment before touching his shoulder hesitantly. "Why do you work for him then?"

"I told you – I owe him."

"You've spent your entire life working for him. Don't you think you've repaid the debt? You could find something else to do with your life."

He laughed jaggedly. "Like what? The only skills I have are using my fists, Mel."

"That isn't true."

"Isn't it?"

"No," she said. "You're a smart guy, Jax. You could do whatever you want with your life."

"You barely know me," he said a bit sullenly.

"I know you're wasting your potential working for a drug dealer like Jimmy Gold – "

"Enough, Mel. Please," he said harshly. "I don't want to talk about Golden while I'm in your bed. Do you understand?"

"Yes."

He paused before putting his arm around her and tugging her against his chest. "I'm sorry. I didn't mean to yell."

"You didn't. Besides, it's none of my business. I'm just being my usual nosy self."

He kissed her forehead. "I like your nosy self."

She pressed her lips against his chest as he relaxed against the headboard. "Do you like being a nurse?"

"I do. I like helping people. Maybe a little too much, sometimes. At least according to my brothers. They could probably use a little less of my 'helping'."

She stared up at him. "I ran into my brother's ex-girlfriend the other day. She said that they broke up because I kept interfering with their relationship."

"Do you believe her?"

She shook her head. "No. She was a lying bitch who cheated on Court numerous times. But I think there's probably some truth to what she said. I spend a lot of time worrying about my brothers even though they're older than me. Well, maybe not so much Court now – Julie's a great woman and perfect for him – but definitely Cal. He's wasting his potential just like you are."

"Maybe it's why we're friends. We've bonded over our mutual lost potential." He grinned at her.

She studied him carefully. "You are friends, aren't you?"

"Yes. At least starting to be."

"Why?"

"What do you mean?"

"Why are you friends with my brother? You have nothing in common."

"Neither do we, yet here we are," he said teasingly.

"We're not friends though, are we?" She said.

A brief look of hurt flickered across his face. "No, I suppose we're not."

"Are you friends with him because you want to be or because Jimmy Golden asked you to be?"

He jerked against her and tried to hide his shock. "Why would you say that?"

"Golden said he had big plans for my brother. Do you know what they are?"

"No," he lied.

"I hate it when you lie to me," she said before pushing out of his arms.

He grabbed her arm before she could leave the bed. "Do we have to talk about this now, Mel? Can't we just enjoy..."

He trailed off and she arched her eyebrow at him, "Fucking each other?"

He nodded and she sighed loudly before allowing him to pull her back into his embrace. "You drive me crazy, Jax Anderson."

He cupped her breast and squeezed it lightly. "Ditto, Melanie Thomas."

Chapter 11

Court stared at the laptop screen. The trailer that served as his office on job sites was hot and stuffy, and he opened the window behind him before wiping the sweat from the back of his neck. He had the start of a headache, two guys had called in sick, and he had a meeting this afternoon that he was dreading.

He glanced at his watch. Julie would be here any minute for lunch and he was looking forward to it more than he could say. He typed a calculation into the spreadsheet and frowned at the results. He'd have to talk to Mark about –

The door to his trailer opened and without looking up, he said, "Hi, honey. Just give me a minute to finish up and I'll be ready for lunch."

"Hello, Court."

He froze before slowly lifting his head and staring at the woman standing in the trailer. She shut the door and stood in front of the desk as he closed his laptop.

"What are you doing here, Janine?"

She gave him a perfect pout before smoothing her hair. "It's good to see you too."

"Get out."

She frowned. "We haven't seen each other in months and that's all you can say to me? Get out?"

"I have nothing else to say to you," he said quietly.

"Please don't be like that, Court. I want to be friends."

He barked harsh laughter. "Since when?"

"I mean it," she said. "I've been thinking a lot about you lately and how badly I screwed us up."

"That's the understatement of the year." He pushed away from the desk and moved toward the door. "Leave, Janine."

"Court, wait!" She hurried after him, placing her hand on his arm and staring up at him. "Just give me a chance to explain, okay?"

"Explain how you ended up riding a bunch of dicks while you were dating me?"

She winced and caressed his arm lightly. "I'm sorry, Court. I want you to know that."

"Good to know," he said.

"I mean it. I really screwed up and I've been wracking my brain for weeks trying to figure out how I can fix this. I miss you and I want a second chance for us."

His mouth dropped open and he gave her a look of stunned disbelief before shaking his head. "You're a real piece of work, aren't you, Janine?"

"Just give me the chance, Court."

"Not a chance in hell. You know I'm with Julie. Don't pretend you don't," he snapped.

"That fat girl your sister was having coffee with the other night?" She said snidely. "C'mon, Court. You think I don't know what you're doing?"

"What the fuck are you talking about?" He asked.

She stepped closer and smiled up at him. "You're trying to make me jealous and, I'll admit, it's kind of working. Although I'm surprised you took such a step down in the looks department. What on earth possessed you to date her? She's pretty enough, I guess, but that body of hers – does she not have any idea how to step away from the dinner table?"

A look of distaste crossed her face. "I'm sure she's a very nice girl but – "

She squealed with surprise when Court grabbed her arm and pushed her up against the wall of the trailer. He stared down at her, his face red and his nostrils flaring and she swallowed thickly.

"Court, calm down."

"I'm perfectly calm, Janine," he said quietly. He leaned down and she stared mesmerized into his eyes as he said, "When I was seven years old, I pushed a girl at school during recess. She scraped her knees and when my father found out what I had done, he spanked me so hard I couldn't sit down for a week. As much as that spanking hurt, my mother's punishment was worse. She told me how wrong I was to hit a girl, how disappointed she was in me, and that if I ever hit a girl again it would break her heart. I vowed that day to never touch a girl in anger again. I couldn't stand the thought of breaking my mother's heart."

"Court…"

He leaned even closer until their faces were only inches apart. "I am dangerously close to breaking my mother's heart today, Janine."

Her face paled. "You wouldn't hit me."

"Stop talking shit about Julie. I love her. Do you understand?"

Janine's eyes widened. "You love her? Are you crazy, Court? You've been dating for what a few weeks? You can't possibly – "

The door opened and Julie, a wicker picnic basket in one hand, stepped into the trailer. "Hey, handsome. Are you ready for…"

She trailed off, staring in surprise at Court and Janine pressed up against the wall of the trailer. "Court? Is - is everything okay?"

Court pushed away from Janine and wrapped his arm around Julie's waist. He kissed her firmly on the mouth before nodding. "Everything's fine, darlin'. Janine was just leaving."

Janine took a step forward, "Court, I – "

"Goodbye, Janine," Court said.

"You're making a mistake," Janine snapped before brushing past them. She slammed the door of the trailer behind her and Julie winced.

"What was that about?" She asked as Court kissed her forehead.

"She wants a second chance," Court said briefly.

"What?" Julie said in disbelief.

"Yeah. I told her not a chance in hell."

She scowled at the floor. "I really dislike her."

"You and me both," Court replied. "Come on, let's eat. I'm starving."

As Julie laid out on the contents of the picnic basket on the round table shoved into the corner of the trailer, Court grabbed two bottles of water from the tiny fridge.

"This looks delicious, darlin'. Thanks."

"You're welcome."

They sat down and Court dug in to the sandwich. He watched Julie toy with her salad before reaching out and touching her hand. "I want nothing to do with Janine, Jules. It's over between us."

"I know," she said.

"Then what's wrong?"

She poked at a piece of lettuce. "Do you ever get tired of hearing people say we can't possibly be in love?"

He nodded. "It's getting a little old. Who did you get it from this time?"

"Mary."

He scowled and she hurried on. "She wasn't trying to be hurtful, she's just worried about me."

"She doesn't have anything to worry about," Court said.

"No, she doesn't." Julie pierced a piece of tomato and popped it into her mouth.

"But?" Court asked.

"But, she made some good - I don't know - observations, I guess."

"Like what?"

"Well, she asked what your favourite colour was, if you were, uh, good with money," she hesitated, "if you wanted kids. And I couldn't answer any of them."

"My favourite colour is grey, I'm pretty frugal with money but you're welcome to look at my bank account, and yes, I want kids."

"Grey isn't a colour," she said.

He laughed loudly and wiped his mouth with a napkin before leaning forward and kissing her firmly. "God, I love you, Jules."

"It isn't," she protested.

"It totally is."

"It totally isn't."

"Well, look at that —we just had our first disagreement," Court said and she rolled her eyes as he bit into an apple.

"Do you want kids, Jules?"

"Yes, very much. Although I'm a little worried that I'll screw them up the way my dad screwed me up," she said.

"You won't, darlin'," he said. "And you're not screwed up."

"You can't know that for sure."

"I do," he said cheerfully. "Do you think Mary is worried that I'm after your money?"

She shrugged. "I don't think so but even if she does, I don't care. I know you're not."

"That's right, little lady. The only thing I'm after is that sweet body of yours." He gave her a lecherous grin and she laughed again.

"Did you speak to the school yet about the architectural program?" Court asked.

She put her fork down and rubbed at her mouth with the back of her hand before staring at the table. "No, I will soon."

"Jules, honey, look at me," he said gently.

She raised her gaze to his face and he took her hand. "Tell me why you keep putting it off."

She sighed and dropped her gaze to the table again, "I'm not sure I want to join the program, Court. It's so far away and I'd have to move. You're busy with work and I'll be busy with classes - we'd never see each other."

He didn't reply and she gave him a nervous look. "What's wrong?"

"Are you not doing this because of me, Jules? Because we'll make it work. I don't want you to give up your dreams because you're afraid of losing me. I'm not going anywhere, darlin'. I swear."

"No, that isn't it," she protested.

"Are you sure? Because I'll drive up there every weekend if I have to. I want you to be happy, Jules," Court said.

"I *am* happy," she said quietly. "I'm happy here with you and I don't want to leave you."

She held up her hand when he started to protest, "It's not just that. I – I don't want to be an architect anymore, Court. I really don't."

"Oh." Court sat back in his chair and Julie gave him an anxious look.

"Are you disappointed in me?"

"What? Of course not. Jules, if you don't want to be an architect that's perfectly fine with me."

"Is it?" She studied him carefully. "You kept pushing me to join the program and I just – well, it made me wonder just a little if you really wanted to be with me. I know that's ridiculous but you're my first boyfriend and I don't have a clue what a healthy or normal relationship should be, and people kept acting so surprised when I said you were encouraging me to go back to school and move away."

He tugged on her hand. "Come here."

She moved around the table, allowing him to pull her down into his lap. He cupped the back of her neck and kissed her again. "I love you, Jules. And truthfully I hated the idea of you moving away. But I want to be the supportive boyfriend and I want you to be happy. I thought going back to school was what you wanted."

She shook her head. "It isn't."

"What do you want?" He asked curiously.

"Well, I want to be a wife and a mom and I – and don't you dare laugh, Court Thomas – I was thinking of volunteering at the Sunshine Seniors Retirement Home. I was looking online and they have a program where you can come in and knit with the seniors. It's more about spending quality time with them and maybe helping them a little with their knitting projects but I've always wanted to do volunteer work. I could also help out at the homeless shelter on Burne Avenue. They're looking for volunteers to help serve dinners on Thursday nights. My dad never wanted me volunteering with the shelters. He said they were full of meth heads and thieves, but I don't think that's true."

"It isn't," Court said.

"Anyway, I don't think I want a career, at least not right now."

Court smiled at her and rubbed her back. "Then do what makes you happy, Jules. That's what makes me happy."

"Are you sure?"

"Yes. Well, and knowing that you're not going to be moving away and I'll have access to those amazing breasts whenever I want."

He squeezed one full breast and she slapped his hand lightly before resting her forehead against his. "Why do you have to be so damn perfect, Court?"

He snorted laughter. "Trust me, darlin'. I'm not."

"No? Name something awful about yourself."

"I leave my dirty clothes on the floor, I never put the toilet seat down, and I may have a severe addiction to Candy Crush."

She laughed and he gave her a solemn look. "I'm serious, Jules. I've been hiding it from you but I play Candy Crush when I'm in the bathroom."

"Oh dear," she said teasingly, "and here I thought you just had unfortunate digestive issues."

"Wow, it feels really good to get that off my chest," he said dramatically. "The secret was tearing me up inside."

She shook her head and kissed his warm mouth. "You're crazy, Court."

"Crazy for you, darlin'. Crazy for you."

Chapter 12

Mel sat down on the couch and rubbed her aching feet. It had been a long shift at the hospital. God, she hated working the day shift and she couldn't wait to be back on evenings. There were more crazies on the night shift but it certainly made the shift go faster. Less time to think about her aching feet and, well, other stuff.

Other stuff being Jax Anderson, sweetheart. Don't try and fool yourself.

Yeah, maybe she had spent the last two days thinking too much about him but hell, she was only human. The sex was ridiculously hot between them, and she was already missing the feel of his hard body pressed between her thighs.

Speaking of which – she rubbed at her sore thigh muscles. Although it had been two days since Jax was in her bed, her leg muscles were still aching. The man had incredible stamina and flexibility and she really needed to get her ass back to yoga if she wanted to keep up with him.

No point, Thomas. You're done sleeping with Jax Anderson, remember?

Yeah, she remembered. She rubbed her feet again as she pushed Jax Anderson out of her head and tried to concentrate on what to make for dinner. Cereal, she decided. She was way too tired to cook. Hell, she didn't even have the energy to order takeout and –

There was a knock on her door and she climbed to her feet, ignoring the dull throb. She checked the peephole before hurriedly opening the door.

"Jax? What are you doing here?"

Jax, standing in the hallway with his hands behind his back, gave her a lazy smile. "I was in the neighbourhood - thought I'd drop by."

"You were in the neighbourhood?" She said skeptically.

"Yes. There's a great Chinese restaurant just two blocks over from here. I go there all the time. It's close to dinner and I thought," he brought his hands out from behind his back and held up the two large paper bags, "you might be hungry."

"That smells really good."

"Invite me in, butterfly."

"Mr. Anderson, won't you please come in?"

* * *

"Oh God, Jax, that feel so good."

"Thirty seconds ago you were complaining that it hurt."

Mel groaned. "I was just being a big baby. God, this is better than sex."

Jax paused with his hands around her foot. "I feel like I should be insulted by that."

She laughed and wiggled her toes. "Don't stop."

"Noodle me."

"What?"

If I have to keep rubbing your feet like you're the queen and I'm your humble and ridiculously well-hung palace slave boy, you're going to have to feed me. Noodle me." He opened his mouth and, grinning like an idiot, Mel dipped her chopsticks into the container of noodles and dropped some noodles into Jax's mouth.

"Thank you, my lady," he mumbled around the noodles as he went back to rubbing the bottom of her feet.

She took her own bite of noodles before pointing the chopsticks at him. "You, Jax Anderson, are nothing like you look."

"No?" He opened his mouth again and she fed him more noodles.

"Definitely not."

"How do I look?" He asked.

"Scary."

He laughed. "I always thought the scar made me look badass."

"It's not the scar, it's just – "

"What?"

"I don't know. You just look scary."

"Like a man who shouldn't be fucked with?" He scowled menacingly at her.

She giggled loudly. "You have a noodle stuck to your face."

His scowl disappeared and he grinned at her before swiping the noodle from his face.

"I feel like you're tough on the outside but actually all marshmallow gooey on the inside," she said.

"I hate marshmallows and I am extremely tough inside and out."

"Says the man with the pet bunnies."

"You can't let that get out to the general public, butterfly. It'll destroy my street cred."

"Your secret is safe with me," she said solemnly before making a zipping motion across her lips. "Do you want more noodles?"

He shook his head and she set the container aside as he continued to rub her foot. She studied him carefully. "In all seriousness, Jax, you're a good guy."

He shook his head and stared moodily at her bare legs. "I'm not a good guy. Don't let the foot rubs and pet bunnies fool you, butterfly."

"Right," she sighed.

They were quiet for a few moments before she gave him a tentative smile. "Do you want to stay and watch a movie or something?"

"I have to be at work in," he checked his watch, "less than two hours."

"Right."

"That doesn't mean we can't do the 'something' though." He grinned at her.

"I could probably find a movie on Netflix that's less than two hours," she pointed out.

"True." He slid his hands up her legs, she was wearing shorts and a t-shirt, and he caressed her soft skin before gripping her thighs and sliding her down the couch toward him. "Or, we could make our own movie."

"Jax Anderson, did you just ask me to make a homemade porno with you?"

He grinned again at her. "You said you did kinky things in the bedroom."

She tugged herself free of his grip and slid off the couch before gathering the containers of food and carrying them into the kitchen. "I'm not making a porno with you, perv."

When she returned from the kitchen he was gone. Where was he? Had she upset him or –

A hard pair of hands circled around her waist and she screamed breathlessly before stomping on the top of Jax's foot.

"Ouch. Easy, butterfly," he grimaced as he tugged her back against him.

"You scared the hell out of me, Jax!" She glared at him over her shoulder and he dropped a kiss on to her lips.

"I'm sorry."

"You don't look sorry," she said.

"I am." He pushed her hair to the side and pressed a kiss on the back of her neck. "Do I need to show you how sorry I am?"

"Maybe," she said.

"It would be my pleasure," he whispered. He tugged her shirt over her head and kissed her back with his warm mouth. He traced her spine with his tongue and she moaned loudly and gripped the back of the couch tightly.

"I've dreamt about your soft skin the last two days, butterfly," he whispered as he unhooked her bra and removed it.

He took off his shirt and pressed his chest against her back as he slid his arms around her and cupped her breasts. He teased her nipples into stiff points, and she moaned quietly when he slid one hand into her shorts and panties and cupped her warmth.

He rubbed her clit until it was wet and swollen and she was grinding her ass against his crotch. He dropped his pants and pushed her forward until she was leaning over the back of the couch. He stroked her ass as she widened her thighs and clutched tightly at the rough fabric of the sofa.

"Hurry, Jax," she said as he ripped open the foil package.

He pushed his finger deep inside of her and she arched her back and thrust back against him. He growled his approval before sliding his finger out and pressing the head of his cock against her. As he slipped into her warmth, he leaned over her and pressed a warm, wet kiss against her bare shoulder.

"I can't stay away from you. I keep trying but – "

"Stop trying," she interrupted.

He kissed her shoulder again. "Whatever you say, butterfly."

* * *

"With all due respect, Mr. Golden, I think you're making a mistake with Jax."

Jimmy leaned back in his chair and stared at Mulroney. "Do you?"

Mulroney nodded. "He's a risk. I know you love him like a son but he won't be a good lieutenant."

"And why do you say that?"

"Just a feeling."

Jimmy laughed loudly and Mulroney's face flushed. "Sir, just hear me out. He doesn't have the smarts to be anything more than your bodyguard. You know that or you wouldn't have kept him in that position for so many years."

"I've kept him where he is because I needed his protection," Jimmy said.

"Exactly. And you need him now more than ever," Mulroney replied. "Chan chopped Johnson's body into fucking pieces as a warning, sir. He's coming after you."

"I can handle Chan."

"Can you?"

"I'm growing tired of you questioning my abilities, Mulroney. Jax is my lieutenant now and you'll treat him with respect and, when necessary, show him the ropes. Do I make myself clear?"

"Sir, I – "

"Do I make myself clear?" Jimmy repeated icily.

"Perfectly," Mulroney snapped.

"Good."

* * *

"You're late," Cal grinned at Jax as he hurried into the nightclub.

"Yeah, I know."

Cal clapped him on the back. "I covered for you. Told Mr. Golden you had texted me and that you were stuck in traffic."

"Thanks."

"No problem. I'm always happy to help out a – "

Cal paused and a brief frown crossed his face as he sniffed at Jax.

"What?" Jax asked.

"Nothing. You'd better get to Mr. Golden's office." Cal walked away.

Chapter 13

"Penny for your thoughts?" Rachel placed a glass of whiskey in front of him and leaned against the counter. Her generous breasts were nearly falling out of her shirt and Jax sighed inwardly.

"Not tonight, Rachel. I'm in no mood."

She scowled at him. "What the hell, Jax? You think because Mr. Golden promoted you that you're too good for me now?"

"Now?" He raised his eyebrow at her and she flushed before straightening.

"You're a real dick, Jax Anderson. You know that?"

"I do." He tipped his glass to her before taking a sip.

She snorted angrily and flounced away as Cal slid on to the stool next to him.

"Bad meeting with Mr. Golden?"

Jax shook his head and stared at the amber-coloured liquid in the glass. They had discussed the location of the next shipment, it was in a week, and he needed to figure out how to get the information to Darvin.

Not that it mattered, he thought bitterly. He and Mulroney were making the drop and without Golden there, the information was useless to the FBI. He might as well just –

"You know, I really couldn't figure out why you were so uninterested in Rachel," Cal said. "She's gorgeous and those tits..."

He trailed off and eyed her chest appreciatively as she stocked the liquor bottles behind the bar.

"I told you – she isn't my type," Jax replied.

"But my sister is?"

Jax jerked on his stool and gave Cal a cautious look. "What the hell are you talking about, Cal?"

Cal laughed. "Don't play dumb with me, buddy. My sister's worn the same perfume for ten years. You think I don't recognize it by now?"

He leaned forward and sniffed at Jax. "You're practically drenched in it."

"Cal, it was just supposed to be a one-time thing but I – "

"Oh, that's supposed to make me feel better?" Cal interrupted. "My sister's only good enough for a one night stand?"

"No! That isn't what I meant and it's more than that, okay? Your sister is – "

"Annoying? Nosy? Always right?"

Jax frowned at him. "She's great, Cal."

Cal nodded. "Yeah, she is. I love her to death and I have to be honest here, Jax – I don't really love the idea of you banging my baby sister."

"She's a grown woman. She can make her own decisions," Jax said tightly.

"She is. And trust me, even if I outright told her not to date you, she wouldn't listen. She doesn't like being told what to do."

"I know."

"How serious are you two?"

Jax didn't reply and Cal frowned. "Don't hurt her, Jax. I know I don't look tough but Court took seven years of boxing and I'm a dirty fighter. You might win in a fight against us but it doesn't mean we won't mess you up."

Jax laughed. "Are you seriously saying that you and Court will beat the shit out of me if I hurt your sister? We're not in high school for fuck's sake, Cal."

Cal grinned at him. "Yeah, I know, but what kind of big brother would I be if I didn't protect my sister?"

"She doesn't need protecting," Jax pointed out.

"True, but she's always worrying about us – I figured it was time to return the favour."

Cal looked Jax up and down. "Truthfully, I never thought we would have to worry about Mel. She's always played it safe, and always dated the good guys."

"You think I'm not a good guy?" Jax asked.

Hurt was trickling in and he pushed it away impatiently. He wasn't a good guy.

Cal shook his head. "I didn't say that. But I do think you're going to break my sister's heart."

He stood and walked away.

* * *

Cal studied the woman who had just entered the nightclub. She was tall and slender with straight blonde hair that fell just past her shoulders. She also looked vaguely familiar and he wondered for a moment if she had ever used his services at the escort agency.

No, he decided. He would remember a woman like her. He hurried forward. "Welcome to the Golden Club. My name is Cal."

He helped her out of her jacket and draped it over his arm, trying not to stare at her body wrapped enticingly in a bright blue dress. "Will you be dining with a party this evening?"

She raised her gaze to his face and his breath stopped in his throat. Her eyes were a clear green and her complexion was pale and perfect.

"No, I'm dining alone."

Her voice sent shivers of need down his spine and he struggled to keep his desire for her from showing on his face.

"Excellent. Let me show you – "

"Hello, Jax."

The woman was looking behind him and Cal turned as a whiff of his sister's perfume filled the air.

"Hello, Jade."

Jax hesitated before leaning down and kissing the woman's cheek. "You look good."

"So do you. It's been a long time," she said.

"I'm surprised to see you here."

She shrugged. "I was close by, thought I'd drop in and see what changes have been made to the place."

She glanced around the club and Cal elbowed Jax in the ribs. He grunted softly and cleared his throat.

"Cal, this is Jade Wilson. Jade, this is Cal Thomas."

"It's nice to meet you." Cal gave her his most charming smile and took her hand. He pressed his mouth against her knuckles before smiling again at her. She was staring at him with a bemused look on her face and she tugged her hand free.

"Forgive me, Ms. Wilson, but you look very familiar," Cal said.

"Do I?" She replied.

"Yes."

"Jade is the district attorney," Jax said. "You've seen her on TV."

Cal's eyes widened and he gave her an admiring look as she stared silently at him.

"It's an honour to have you here," Cal said.

He gave Jade's jacket to the coat attendant before extending his arm toward Jade. "I think the best table in the house and a complimentary glass of wine is in order."

"That won't be necessary." She took his arm and Cal led her toward one of the more private tables. Jax was following them and he glanced behind him and gave him his best 'get lost' look. Jax rolled his eyes but continued to follow.

"Here you are, Ms. Wilson." He pulled out her chair and unfolded her napkin, placing it on her lap as she picked up the wine menu.

"Why don't you join me, Jax," Jade said.

Cal frowned. Was there something going on between Jax and the district attorney?

"Thank you, but I'd better not."

Jade laughed bitterly. "Of course. It would probably upset the old man."

"No," Jax said immediately. "You know he'd be fine with us having dinner but I'm working and – "

"Still defending him, huh?" Jade laughed again as Cal's frown deepened. "Doesn't matter what he does or says, you'll always have his back. Won't you, Jax?"

"This is neither the time nor the place," Jax said quietly.

"No, I suppose not."

Jax hesitated before touching her shoulder. "What are you doing here, Jade? This isn't a good idea."

"What do you know of good ideas? You still work for him, remember? At least I was smart enough to get away."

"Jade, he's – "

"Jade?"

Jimmy's voice echoed through the nightclub and Cal turned to see the old man hurrying toward them. He stopped beside the table, an unfamiliar look of nervousness crossing his face, before holding out his hand.

"It's good to see you, Jade."

She stared at his outstretched hand and he dropped it to his side. "What are you doing here?"

She shrugged. "I'm not allowed to be here?"

"Of course you are. I'm just surprised, that's all," Jimmy said.

"I bet you are," she replied.

Jimmy glanced at Jax and Jade laughed. "Don't worry, Jimmy. I'm done trying to help Jax see the truth about you."

"I'm your father, Jade, and you'll address me as such," Jimmy snapped.

Cal's mouth dropped open and he shut it with a snap as Jimmy leaned over the table. "And tell your damn FBI watchdogs to leave me the hell alone."

"I don't know what you're talking about."

Jimmy snorted. "I mean it, Jade."

"Sorry, Jimmy, you don't get to tell me what to do anymore," Jade said softly.

Jimmy's face turned red and he clamped his hands around the edge of the table. "Always with the smart mouth. You'd better watch yourself or you'll find your tongue ripped out of that smart mouth."

Jax grabbed his arm and tugged him upright. "Enough, sir."

Jade stared defiantly at her father as he breathed heavily for a moment before nodding. "You're right, Jax, of course you are."

He turned to Jade. "It was good to see you again, Jade. Have a glass of wine on me."

He stalked away as Jax placed a hand on Jade's shoulder. She jerked away. "Don't touch me, Jax."

"Jade, you shouldn't – "

"Shouldn't what?" She interrupted? "Shouldn't goad him? Why the hell not? He spent years making my life hell, I deserve a little payback."

She stood up as Mulroney joined them. "Jax? We need to go. There's an errand we need to run for Mr. Golden."

"Just give me a minute," Jax said. "Jade – "

"This was a bad idea," she muttered before storming past the three men. Jax groaned under his breath and Cal hesitated before chasing after her. Holding her coat over one arm, she pushed out of the club. Cal followed her, grabbing her arm and pulling her to a stop in front of the door.

"Let go of me," she frowned at him.

"Are you okay?" He studied her face. Her cheeks were red with fury and she tossed her head impatiently before glaring at him.

"I'm perfectly fine. Let go of my arm."

"Not until you calm down," Cal said. "You shouldn't drive like this."

"Who are you? My mother?" She snapped. "I don't need your help."

He smiled charmingly at her. "Humour me then, okay?"

She stared up at him. "You think you can just smile at me and get me to do what you want?"

"It usually works on the ladies," he said.

"Tell me, Mr....?"

"Thomas, Cal Thomas."

"Tell me, Mr. Thomas, do you ever date women with any brains in their pretty little heads?"

He shrugged. "I dated a senator once. She dumped me for her personal trainer. Apparently I was too smart for her."

She stared at him and he smiled again when her lips twitched. "Admit it, Ms. Wilson. You find me charming."

"I don't even know you."

"That's true. Why don't I take you for coffee this week, and we can get to know each other better?"

"Not a chance. I don't date men who are prettier than I am."

He laughed. "I know you're trying to insult me but considering that you're drop-dead gorgeous, I'll take that as a compliment."

She pressed her lips together in an effort not to laugh and tugged on his hand. "Let me go."

The door opened and Jax and Mulroney joined them. Jax gave her a worried look. "Jade, are you okay?"

"I'm just fine, Jax," she snapped.

A car pulled up in front of the club and a man stepped out. Cal studied the automatic weapon in his hand with numb surprise. Why the hell did he have a gun? Was that type of weapon even allowed in the –

"Cal! GET DOWN!" Jax shouted as the man raised the gun.

Moving instinctively, Cal shoved Jade to the ground and dove on top of her as the man opened fire. The gunfire was deafening and dimly he was aware of Jade's cry of fear under him as Mulroney screamed piercingly.

Mulroney was thrown backwards against the wall, blood pouring from the multiple bullet wounds to his chest and torso. He started to slide down the wall, already dead, and Jax cursed loudly and grabbed his body, using it as a shield as the man opened fire on him. He grunted in pain when a bullet went through Mulroney and lodged in his left shoulder. It spun him around and he slammed into the door before sinking to his knees. He fell forward, blood pouring from his shoulder, as the man moved toward Cal and Jade.

"I'm going to let you live." The man had a thick accent and he pointed the gun at Jade. "So that you may give Mr. Chan's regards to Golden."

"Wait," Cal said. "You don't have to – "

The man turned the gun on him and Cal flinched when the shot rang out. The man stiffened and glanced down at his chest. Blood was blooming on his shirt and he touched it lightly before holding his fingers out accusingly to Cal.

"What the fuck?" Cal whispered.

The man sank to his knees and Cal stared wide-eyed at Jax standing behind him and holding a gun in his right hand. Blood had soaked through his shirt and Cal's eyes widened when he pressed the muzzle against the man's temple.

"Jax, wait! Don't – "

Jade screamed sharply and Cal flinched again when Jax shot the man in the head. He fell forward, his face smacking into the pavement, and Jax staggered back. He was panting harshly and Jade cried out when he tripped over the body of Mulroney and fell to the ground.

"Jax!" She wormed out from under Cal and crawled over to Jax. She pressed her hand against the wound on his shoulder.

"You're going to be okay, honey. Just stay awake, okay?"

He nodded weakly and she glared at Cal over her shoulder. "Don't just fucking sit there! Call 9-1-1!"

Chapter 14

Court sat up in bed and rubbed at his eyes before reaching for his ringing cell phone. He stared blearily at the number and groaned before answering it.

"Do you have any idea what fucking time it is, Cal?"

Julie stirred beside him and he rubbed her back lightly as he yawned. "Slow down, Cal. I can't understand a word you're saying."

Julie sat up and turned on the bedside lamp as Court suddenly stiffened.

"Shot? What the fuck? Are you okay?"

Julie stared wide-eyed at him as he listened silently for a moment. "Are you sure you're okay? Jesus, Cal. No, I'll be right there, just hang tight, okay?"

He hesitated before frowning. "Mel? Why would I tell Mel?"

His eyes widened. "You're fucking kidding me! Jesus Christ, what the hell is happening?"

Julie squeezed his leg reassuringly as he ran his hand through his short hair. "Okay, yeah, I'll tell her. No, I'll swing by her apartment and pick her up. If what you said is true, then I don't want her driving. The last thing we need is for her to get in an accident. I'll see you soon, Cal. I love you."

He hung up the phone and Julie gave him a worried look. "What happened?"

"There was a, well, an incident, at the club tonight. Some guy shot at a few of Mr. Golden's employees."

"Cal?" Julie said anxiously.

"He's fine. At least I think he is. He sounded really fucking freaked out but he was right there when it happened, he said. He didn't give me the details, just said that a guy was dead and Jax was in surgery," Court said as he slipped out of bed and picked up his jeans from the floor.

"Oh my God!" Julie climbed out of bed and dressed hurriedly.

"Honey, it's the middle of the night. You don't have to go with me," Court said.

She shook her head. "Of course I'm going with you."

Court pulled a shirt over his head. "I have to stop at Mel's. Apparently she's dating Jax."

"Oh?" Julie was wiggling into her bra and he studied her pink cheeks.

"You knew, didn't you?"

She pressed her lips together before yanking a sweater over her head. "Mel and I had talked about it."

"You didn't tell me," Court said.

"Because your sister asked me not to," she replied.

"Jax is dangerous."

"You don't know that. You barely know him," she said gently.

He sighed and grabbed his phone off the bed. Julie took his hand and he squeezed it firmly as they left his bedroom.

* * *

Cal stepped out into the hospital parking lot. The air was cold and he pulled his jacket around him as he searched the lot. There was no sign of her and he walked around the building. She was standing against the wall, holding a book of matches and cursing loudly.

He stood beside her and plucked the matches from her trembling fingers. "You shouldn't smoke. It's bad for you."

"Is it? I had no idea," she snapped irritably.

She didn't resist when he took the cigarette from her. He stuck it in his mouth and lit it with a match, inhaling deeply and blowing the smoke out before handing her the cigarette. She took a drag and he patted her on the back when she coughed wretchedly.

"Fuck," she sighed. "Made it four goddamn months this time." She inhaled again and then passed the cigarette to him. He took his own drag as she stared at the ground.

"Is he dead?" Her voice was low and thick with tears.

He shook his head. "No. He's out of surgery and in recovery right now. They got the bullet out. He'll be pretty sore and will have to do physiotherapy but he'll live."

"Thank God," she breathed as tears rolled down her cheeks.

"You love him," he said quietly.

"Of course I do," she said as she wiped the tears away and took the cigarette back.

"I hate to tell you this but he's, uh, dating my sister."

She gave him an irritated look. "Jax is like a brother to me, Mr. Thomas."

"Oh." He ignored the rush of relief that went through him. "You should probably get checked out. I wasn't exactly gentle when I shoved you to the ground."

"I'm fine." She hesitated. "Thanks by the way. It was very heroic of you to cover me with your body."

He grinned at her. "I guess this gets me at least one coffee date, yeah?"

She rolled her eyes. "This is hardly the time for flirting, Mr. Thomas."

"Yeah, you're probably right. Why don't we just go back to your place and have crazy survivor sex?"

"Excuse me?" She paused with the cigarette halfway to her mouth.

He took it and inhaled deeply before blowing out smoke rings. "Survivor sex. It's where two people who have a near-death experience together have crazy hot sex with each other."

"Tempting, but no," she said before taking back the cigarette. She took a drag and then crushed it under her heel.

"I'm going to check on Jax."

"Are you sure you want to do that? Your father will probably be there."

She laughed bitterly. "If you actually believe he'll show up at this hospital, you're a fool. He'll be too busy worrying about his own skin to care about Jax."

"That isn't true. Jax is like a son to him."

"Doesn't matter. He won't risk it."

"Who is Chan?" Cal asked.

"My father is a drug dealer," she said abruptly.

"I know."

Her eyes widened. "What? How do you know? Are you in his inner circle?"

"No. But I'm not stupid. I hear things and see things."

"What things?" She asked eagerly. "What things do you see and hear?"

"Nothing that will help you put your father in prison."

"I'm going to get him, you know. I'm going to end his goddamn drug empire and watch him rot in prison for the rest of his life."

He didn't reply and she gave another bitter laugh. "You think I'm a horrible person. Don't you, Cal?"

"No."

"You should get out while you still can," she warned him. "If you're not careful he'll drag you into the mud with him, and a pretty boy like you won't do well in prison."

"Thanks for the tip."

"You're welcome." She pushed past him.

"They won't let you see him. Only family is allowed in the ICU," he called after her.

"I'm his sister," she replied softly.

* * *

"Open your eyes, honey."

Jax groaned and shifted in the bed. It sent a bolt of pain up his left side and he groaned again.

"Don't do that, Jax. Don't move, just open your eyes for me."

He wanted to ignore her. He wanted to return to floating in the darkness, plagued by neither pain nor bad dreams, but her voice was insistent. Finally, his need to see her won over his desire to return to the black, and he forced his eyelids open.

"Butterfly?"

"Hey, handsome."

'What are you doing here?"

"Oh you know, I heard you were shot and figured I didn't want to miss all the fun of watching you recover from surgery," she said.

He turned his head and stared at his bandaged shoulder before eyeing the machines that beeped and blinked. "How did you get in here?"

She smiled. "I work here, remember? I called in some favours."

She leaned over him and petted his hair before whispering in his ear, "I'm known as the Godfather at the hospital."

He laughed and then groaned in pain. She sat back and rubbed his chest.

"I'm sorry, honey."

"Is Cal okay?" Oddly, he couldn't remember much of what happened after he was shot.

"He's fine," she said. "He's here but they won't let him in the ICU."

"I'm sorry," he whispered.

She stroked his forehead. "For what?"

"I don't know. Dragging you here in the middle of the night."

She shook her head. "I don't mind. I'm just glad that you're alive."

"Me too." He reached for her hand with his good one and she linked her fingers with his.

"It scared the hell out of me when Court and Julie knocked on my door. I was so afraid that I'd never see you again and that I ..."

She trailed off and he squeezed her hand. "What?"

"Nothing. It's not important," she said. "Do you have any idea how lucky you were, Jax? Cal said that another man died and that he would have died too if you hadn't saved him."

He didn't reply and she pressed her mouth against his. "Thank you for saving his life."

"Kiss me again," he whispered.

She shook her head. "You need to concentrate on healing."

"Pretty sure the kissing helps."

She laughed. "Really? Maybe I should start kissing all of my patients then."

"Don't you dare, butterfly. I'm the only one you should be kissing."

"Is that right?" She whispered as she bent her head toward him.

"Yes," he murmured.

She pressed her lips against his as a voice said, "Jax?"

Mel sat back and stared at the woman standing at the end of the bed. She was slender with blonde hair and she clutched nervously at her jacket as she stared at Jax.

"How are you feeling, honey?"

Mel frowned at the endearment as Jax squeezed her hand reassuringly. "I'll live, Jade."

Even her name was gorgeous. Mel swallowed down her jealousy as Jade moved around the bed and pressed a kiss on Jax's forehead. "Thank God."

Jax smiled faintly at her. "Jade, this is Mel Thomas. Mel, this is Jade Wilson – my sister."

"It's nice to meet you," Mel said politely.

"Your Cal's sister?"

"I am," she confirmed.

A small smile crossed Jade's face. "He's very charming."

"He certainly tries to be," Mel replied and the smile on Jade's face grew.

"Well, I'll leave you two alone. I just wanted to check on you." She squeezed Jax's arm. "I'm going home."

"You shouldn't be alone," Jax said.

She shook her head. "I'll be fine, honey. It's not me they're after."

She kissed him once more before smiling at Mel. "It was nice to meet you, Mel. Take good care of my brother."

"I will," she replied.

* * *

Jax held the juice bottle between his legs and twisted open the cap with one hand. His left arm was still in the sling and he grunted irritably when the juice spilled over on to his hand. He licked it away and poured some into the glass.

It had been nearly a week since the shooting and while the pain was diminishing, his left arm was still useless. He flexed it gingerly, wincing at the pain, and downed the juice in three swallows. He hated being injured, hated feeling like an invalid, and the only bright spot in the whole goddamn mess was Melanie. She had come over every day after work, spending the nights with him and cooking his meals, feeding Ricky and Lucy, and helping him shower and dress. Having her with him had been – well, it had been fucking amazing if he was being truthful – and despite the pain, this was the happiest he'd ever been. He had a sneaking suspicion that he was starting to fall in love with her and even though he knew it was dangerous, he was helpless to stop.

She had shown up after work today, looking uncharacteristically tired, but had kissed him sweetly before heading for the shower. He cocked his head and listened. The shower was still running and he wondered what she would say if he joined her. He had tried a few times to make love to her but she had refused, saying that he needed more time to heal. He grinned to himself and started toward the stairs. She would find it more difficult to resist if he was naked and in the shower with her.

The doorbell rang and, frowning, he walked to the front door and answered it. A man with a picture of a steaming slice of pizza on the front of his shirt held out a cardboard box.

"Pizza's here."

"I didn't order a pizza." Jax started to close the door and the man stuck his foot out to block it.

"Sure you did."

"No, I didn't."

"Yes, you did," the man said pointedly.

Jax frowned before digging his wallet out of his back pocket. "How much do I owe you?"

"Twenty."

He handed the man the bills and shoved his wallet back into his pocket before taking the pizza box from him. The man tipped his hat to him. "Have a great day, sir."

He sauntered down the sidewalk and Jax closed the door and carried the pizza box into the kitchen. He set it on the counter and stared fixedly at it. After a few seconds it rang shrilly and, wincing, he flipped the lid up. The box held no pizza but did have a small cell phone taped to the bottom of it. He pulled it free and checked the stairs before answering it.

"Hello, Jax. How are you feeling?" Agent Darvin asked.

"Like I've been shot." He moved into the office and shut the door firmly. "What do you want?"

"The drop location and date."

"Tomorrow night at the warehouse by the wharf."

"The abandoned one?"

"Yes."

"Good," Agent Darvin said in a pleased voice.

"It's useless information, Darvin," Jax said.

"It isn't. Mulroney is dead."

There was glee in Darvin's voice and Jax snarled into the phone, "Mulroney had a family. He might have been a goddamn drug dealer but he had a wife and two little girls who are growing up without their goddamn father. So maybe you could keep the fucking delight out of your voice. What do you say, Agent Darvin?"

There was a moment of silence before Darvin cleared his voice. "You're right. I'm sorry, Jax."

"It doesn't matter anyway. Golden isn't doing the drop. I am," Jax said wearily.

"No, you're not."

"He already talked to me about it. I'm going alone. He doesn't care that I'm injured."

"Shocking," Darvin said dryly. "You're not going, Jax. We have a plan."

"We?"

"The FBI and Ms. Wilson, of course."

"Of course. Listen, do me a favour and tell Jade not to repeat her little stunt at the restaurant. She keeps showing up there and Golden's going to get suspicious."

"She was doing it to try and thwart any of his suspicions, Jax. She thought, and we agreed, that if she showed Golden there was tension between the two of you, it would help end his suspicion of you."

"He isn't suspicious of me."

"Maybe, maybe not," Darvin said. "It doesn't matter anyway."

"Doesn't matter? Jade almost fucking died!" Jax snarled again.

Darvin sighed. "Jax, I know this has been rough on you but we're at the finish line. Just listen to the plan, okay?"

Jax grunted in reply and listened silently as Darvin talked for nearly five minutes. Nausea was growing in his stomach and he sat down in the chair as Darvin finally stopped speaking.

"Well, what do you think?" Darvin asked after a few seconds of silence.

"I can't do it."

"What do you mean you can't do it?" Darvin asked. "It's a good plan, Jax."

"I just can't, okay?" He glanced at the door. It was Mel he was thinking of. If he followed through with this plan he would never see her again.

"You don't have a choice, Jax. If you ever want to get out of this life, you need to do it," Darvin said slowly. "There's a whole lot of money and a warm beach with your name on it waiting for you. You cannot back out on us now. Do you hear me?"

"There has to be another way," Jax said.

"There isn't. You know there isn't. It's happening tomorrow night. Be walking out of Harper's grocery store at eight. Golden won't have enough time to cancel the drop and he'll have to do it himself."

Jax stayed silent and Darvin cleared his throat. "I know about your relationship with Cal Thomas' sister."

"How the fuck do you know that?"

"Ms. Wilson told us. If you care about her, you'll do this now. Sooner or later Golden will find out about her and then she's going to be hurt. Either by someone trying to get to you or by Golden himself."

"You don't know that."

"I do, and so do you," Darvin said firmly. "Tomorrow morning at nine, there will be a dry cleaning service knocking at your door. The suit bag will have everything you need."

Jax didn't reply and Darvin sighed loudly. "You need to do this, Jax. You'll never be free of him if you don't."

"Yeah," he grunted. "I have to go."

"Are we on for tomorrow night or not, Jax? I need to know. We have a lot to set up in the next twenty-four hours."

"Yes!" Jax snapped. "I have to go!"

He hung up and threw the phone in the small wastebasket with enough force to tip it over. He rubbed his hand across his forehead and jerked in his chair when Mel said, "Who was that?"

He looked up. Mel was standing in the doorway wearing jeans and a t-shirt. Her hair was wet and she combed it nervously with her fingers as she stared at him.

"Who was that, Jax?"

"No one," he muttered before swiveling his chair and staring out the window at the darkness.

"You're lying to me."

He swallowed thickly. He had been a fool to think he could have a relationship with Mel. Being with him would eventually get her killed. His stomach rolled again with nausea as an image of Mel, her body broken and bleeding in some cold ditch, flickered through his mind. Agent Darvin was right. He was putting Mel in terrible danger and he would never forgive himself if she was hurt or killed. He took a deep breath and steeled himself to break his butterfly's heart.

"Jax? Don't ignore me."

He turned around and scowled at her. "Do you ever get tired of accusing me of lying?"

She twitched backwards before giving him her own scowl. "Do you ever get tired of lying to me?"

He stood in front of her and, making his voice deliberately harsh, said, "Maybe if you weren't so damn nosy about everything, I wouldn't have to lie."

She recoiled as if he had struck her and gave him a look of pain that stabbed him directly in the heart. "You son of a bitch."

"This isn't working," he said.

"What? What the hell are you talking about, Jax?"

"I've made a mistake. I can't be with someone like you."

"Someone like me? What, someone who actually fucking cares about you? Who worries about you?"

"Someone who constantly hovers. Who thinks she can control me."

"I'm not trying to control you!" She shouted.

"You are, and I'm tired of it. I think you should leave, Mel."

She stared in shock at him before snarling, "You fucking asshole!"

She turned and ran from the office. He stayed where he was, clenching his fist and struggling not to go after her as she gathered her stuff and stormed out of his life forever. The front door slammed and he sank to the ground, burying his face in his trembling hand as his stomach churned.

Chapter 15

He showed up the next afternoon, ringing the doorbell repeatedly until Jax finally opened the door and stared wearily at him.

"You look like shit, Jax."

"Good to see you too, Cal. Did you bring your brother to kick my ass?"

"Let me in."

"No."

"Let me in, asshole. We need to talk," Cal snapped.

"No, we don't."

"I told you not to hurt her, Jax. Do you remember that conversation?"

"It's none of your business, Cal."

"Oh yes it fucking is. What the fuck is going on with you, Jax? One minute you're playing house with my sister and the next minute you're kicking her out of your life. Did you not care about her at all?"

"I said it wasn't any of your business. Go away," Jax said.

"You owe her an explanation."

Jax glared at him. "What do you want me to say, Cal? That I finally came to my senses and realized how bad I was for her? We almost died less than a fucking week ago. What if Mel had been there? Did you think about that? What if she had been there to see me and that fucking asshole Chan hired had killed her? She isn't safe with me and you know it! I'm not good enough for her!"

"Jax, you can't – "

"Leave me alone, Cal," Jax said. "I made a mistake and I'm sorry I hurt Melanie but I can't change the past."

Cal stared silently at him before shaking his head. "You're such a fucking idiot that you don't even realize you're making the biggest mistake of your life. But you're right about one thing – you're not good enough for her."

He walked to his car and drove away as Jax shut the door and stared at the black suit bag hanging on the hook in the hallway. He was doing the right thing so why did it feel so wrong?

* * *

"Al, we forgot the potatoes."

"We didn't forget the potatoes, Marjorie."

"I'm telling you we did." The woman, she was in her late sixties with short grey hair, stopped at the door and began to rummage through the shopping bags she held.

"We can't leave here without the potatoes. Todd loves potatoes and I want his birthday dinner to be special. He's our only boy and he – "

Al sighed and ran his hand through his own grey hair. "I distinctly remember buying them, Marjorie."

"Then the cashier forgot to give them to us. Be a dear and run back to the till, would you?"

"Are you sure they're not at the bottom of the bag?"

"Oh for heaven's sake!" Marjorie gave him an exasperated look. "I know what a bag of potatoes looks like, Al. I'm telling you – they're not in here."

Al continued to hesitate and she said irritably, "Fine, I'll do it myself."

She turned to march back to the till and nearly ran into the tall, dark-haired man standing behind her. He was wearing a thick jacket, the left sleeve swung empty, and she could see the strap of a hospital sling around his neck. She studied the scar that ran from his temple down his throat.

"Oh! I'm so sorry!" She took a step back, eyeing him nervously.

He nodded in acknowledgement and skirted around her before pushing open the door and leaving the store. She stared after him for a moment as Al made a noise of impatience

"Marjorie, are you going back to the till or not? There's a new 'Cops' on tonight and I'm going to miss it if we don't – "

There was a loud bang from outside the store and Marjorie let loose with a shrill scream as the large glass window in the front of the grocery store exploded with a jagged cough. There was another round of gunfire, this one even louder than the first, and the man with the scar was driven back through the broken window. He landed with a hard thump on the tile floor and Marjorie screamed again when blood pooled beneath his body.

A crowd of people were gathering and a man fought his way through them.

"Let me through! I'm a doctor!" He shouted.

The crowd parted and the man kneeled beside the scarred man. The pool of blood had grown and the man wasn't moving. The doctor pressed his fingers against the man's throat and Marjorie gave Al a horrified look when he shook his head.

"He's dead."

* * *

"Come in!" Jimmy barked irritably.

The door to his office opened and Cal walked in. His face was pale and his mouth trembling and Jimmy frowned at him. "What the hell is wrong with you? You look like you've seen a ghost."

"Mr. Golden, I – "

"Never mind, I don't have time for this shit," Jimmy said. "Where the fuck is Jax? He was supposed to be here twenty goddamn minutes ago."

"Mr. Golden," Cal whispered, "There's been a..."

He trailed off and Jimmy gave him an impatient look. "What the fuck, Thomas? Spit it out already."

"Jax is dead," Cal said bluntly.

Jimmy froze before slumping back in his chair. "What happened?"

He was shot just outside of a grocery store on the south side. He – there was a doctor in the store but Jax died immediately."

Cal rubbed his mouth with a trembling hand as Jimmy stared blankly at him.

"Mr. Golden? Are you – "

"Get out."

"Mr. Golden, maybe I should call someone for you?"

"Get. Out." Jimmy said slowly.

When Cal didn't move, Jimmy shouted, "Get the fuck out!"

"Yes, sir." Cal closed the door and Jimmy sat quietly for a moment before with a loud scream of rage he sent the stuff on his desk crashing to the floor with a sweep of his arm.

He sat back and stared at the ceiling for nearly two minutes before sitting forward and picking up his cell phone from the floor. He would mourn the death of Jax later. He had less than half an hour until the drop and he had no one to deliver it.

For a moment he considered sending Cal before cursing under his breath. The pretty boy would shit his pants if he delivered a shipment to his new clients. They weren't exactly model citizens and, besides, he couldn't trust Cal. He barely knew him. He had trusted Jax and he had trusted Mulroney and now both of them were dead less than a week apart. He didn't have a choice – he would have to make the drop himself.

"Fucking Chan," he suddenly muttered, "When I'm done with you, you're going to wish your mother had never spread her legs for your fuckhead of a father."

* * *

Mel looked up from the nurses' station. "Cal? What are you doing here?"

"Is there somewhere private we can talk, Mel?" Cal was white as a ghost and he was rubbing compulsively at his mouth.

"What's wrong?" She hurried around the desk and grabbed his arm. "What's wrong, Cal?"

"Somewhere private, please, Mel," he said hoarsely.

She led him into a supply room and shut the door. "You're scaring me, Cal."

"Something bad has happened, Mel," he said.

Her eyes widened, "Are mom and dad okay?"

"They're fine."

"Court, is he – "

"He's fine too," he interrupted. "It's Jax."

"What about him?" She whispered.

"He's gone, Mel. I'm so sorry."

"What do you mean, he's gone?"

"He — he's dead. He was shot outside of a grocery store earlier tonight."

"No." She staggered back and Cal rushed forward and caught her as her knees buckled.

"No!" She shouted and hit him in the chest with her fists. "That isn't funny, Cal! He's not dead!"

"He is, Mel. I'm so sorry, but he is," Cal said.

She stared blankly at him before bursting into tears. He pushed her head against her chest and kissed the top of her head.

"I'm so sorry," he whispered repeatedly as she buried her face in her hands and sobbed.

* * *

Jimmy opened the trunk of his car and removed a large leather bag. Holding it tightly, he took a quick glance around before walking quickly into the empty warehouse. He blinked and held his hand up when a flashlight shone in his face.

"Get that fucking light out of my face," he snapped.

The light clicked out and a moment later, the warehouse was filled with dim light as his client turned on the headlights of his car.

"Mr. Golden, I didn't expect to see you personally delivering." The man, he was dark-haired with a swarthy complexion, leaned against the car. There were two other men with him, both of them covered in tattoos, and they watched with bored expressions on their faces as Jimmy walked toward them.

"There was a problem with my associates," Jimmy said.

"I heard."

"Did you?" Jimmy said.

"Yes. News travels fast in this city. Don't you think?"

"Do you have my money?" Jimmy asked impatiently.

"Do you have my product?"

Jimmy unzipped the bag and showed the man the contents. It was filled to the brim with packets of white powder and the man smiled before reaching for it. Jimmy pulled it back.

"Money first."

"Of course. You will, I assume, be sticking around while we ensure the product is good," the man said.

"It's good," Jimmy grunted.

"I'm sure it is. But we're still going to check. It'll give you time to count the cash." The man nodded to his two companions. The first moved to the trunk of the car and pulled out a briefcase as the second one casually moved his jacket back to reveal the gun tucked into his waistband.

Jimmy rolled his eyes but said nothing as he exchanged bags with the man. He watched as the man set the bag on the hood of his car and withdrew a package of the fine white powder.

"Is this really necessary? You know the product is – "

"FBI! Don't move!"

Jimmy reached for the gun in the holster at his waist as a dozen FBI agents, dressed all in black and carrying automatic weapons, surrounded them.

"Hands up! Don't move!" They screamed repeatedly.

With an angry snarl, Jimmy lifted his hands as the agents quickly subdued the other men.

As one of the armed agents handcuffed his hands behind his back, a man in a dark suit approached him, smiling benignly. "Hello, Mr. Golden."

"Agent Darvin, you're looking well."

"Thank you." The man straightened his suit sleeves. "It's a new suit. Figured I'd dress up for such a special occasion."

"You know my lawyers will have me out in less than three hours, Agent Darvin. Just like always."

"Not this time, Mr. Golden," Agent Darvin said softly. "And you know it."

Jimmy cleared his throat, "You have no idea – "

"Oh, I think he does," a soft voice said behind him.

He craned his head and stared at the woman as she smiled at him. "Hello, dad."

"Arresting your own father is a new low for you, Jade."

"Actually, I consider it my biggest triumph," she said.

"How did you know I would be here?" He asked suddenly.

"You don't need to know the details. It's not going to help you when I put you in prison for the rest of your miserable life."

He gave her a tight smile, "I'll never spend a single night in prison, Jade."

She smiled again. "We both know that isn't true."

She started to walk away and he shouted after her, "Jade! Wait – I can make you a deal! I have plenty of information and I'll – "

She turned and put her finger against her lips. "No, Jimmy. No deals."

"You can't do this to me! I'm your father!" He snarled angrily.

She studied him silently for a moment. "Good-bye, dad."

She walked out of the warehouse, a smile of triumph on her lips.

Chapter 16

"It's over," Jade said softly. "You should be happy, honey. In three days, you'll be living your new life."

"Yeah," Jax stared out the window of the safe house. His arm was throbbing dully and he rubbed gingerly at his chest. The bullet proof vest had saved his life after Agent Darvin shot him outside of the grocery store but it had left a hell of a bruise.

"Why did you go to the FBI?" Jade asked. "You never did say."

"The hell of it is, there wasn't one single reason," he said. "I just, I don't know, was tired of the game. Tired of watching him hurt people, tired of him making *me* hurt people, and I wanted to be free."

She didn't reply and he gave her a guilty look. "Your father saved my life."

She shook her head impatiently. "Maybe that's true and maybe it isn't – we'll never know. But saving your life doesn't mean you owe him your life, Jax. You have nothing to feel guilty about. He was a terrible man who did terrible things and what you did was the right thing to do."

"Yeah," he muttered.

"I know you miss her," Jade said.

He turned and sat across from her at the small kitchen table. "I do."

"We could tell her. Now that Jimmy's behind bars, we could tell her the truth."

He laughed bitterly. "What good would that do? I'm leaving, remember?"

"You'll be back for the trial."

"In a year or two," he said. "Am I supposed to ask her to just wait for me? Or, hell, I know – maybe I could ask her to go with me. How do you think that conversation would go?"

"Jax – "

"Hey, Mel. I know we've just met but would you like to leave your family and friends, your job, your entire fucking life, and go into witness protection with me?"

"Honey, she might – "

"She might what, Jade?" Jax asked wearily. "She might say yes? There's no fucking way she will. It's better for her if she believes I'm dead, just like everyone else."

"Maybe you should give her the chance to make that decision for herself," Jade said.

He shook his head. "No. It's better this way."

"Jax – "

"I'm tired, Jade. I'm going to lie down for a while."

He left the kitchen and Jade chewed at her bottom lip for a moment before pulling out her cell phone. She did a quick Google search and, with a nervous glance behind her, punched in the number.

The phone rang in her ear and she waited patiently until he answered.

"Hey, pretty boy. It's Jade. I was wondering if you wanted to have that coffee?"

* * *

Cal parked in front of the small grey-coloured house and locked the car before starting up the sidewalk. The door opened and he smiled at Jade. "Hello, beautiful."

"Hey, come on in for a minute."

He followed her into the house and stared curiously at the sparse furnishings. "I like your place?"

She laughed. "It's not my house, Cal."

"Okay, so why are we here?"

"I've got something I need to tell you. Something important."

"Sure, what is it?"

"Well..."

"Jade? I can't find the fucking juice. I thought you said it was in the fridge but there isn't..."

Jax stood in the doorway to the kitchen and stared silently at Cal before clearing his throat. "Hello, Cal."

"Holy fuck," Cal breathed.

* * *

Mel screeched to a stop behind Cal's car and jumped out of her car. She ran up the sidewalk, her heart thudding loudly in her chest, and gave Cal a look of fear as he opened the door of the grey house.

"Cal? What's wrong?"

"Nothing's wrong, Mel. Just come in for a minute, okay?"

"You said it was an emergency."

"Yeah, I kind of said that to get you out of the house."

"Asshole," she muttered as she followed him into the house. "What is this place?"

"Come into the kitchen."

She followed him down the narrow hallway into the kitchen and blinked in surprise when she saw Jade sitting at the table.

"Hello, Melanie."

"Hello, Jade. What are you doing here?"

"Will you sit down? We need to talk."

Frowning, Mel sat down in the chair across from her. Cal pulled up a chair next to her and took her hand as Jade smiled nervously at her.

"Jimmy Golden's been arrested."

"Yeah, I saw it on the news," Mel replied. She swallowed past the lump in her throat and rubbed at her forehead. She had spent most of the last two days crying wretchedly and her skull was throbbing and aching.

"He's going to prison for a long time. We caught him delivering the drugs himself," Jade said.

"I guess that means you're out of a job," Mel said to Cal. "What are you going to do now?"

He shrugged. "You know me, I always find something."

"Right," she muttered. "Listen, I'm sorry, maybe you think I'd be happy that Jimmy Golden is behind bars and I guess I am, but I don't get why you had to drag me over here just to tell me that."

"There's more, Melanie," Jade said gently. "Jax was working with the FBI to bring Golden down. It's because of him that we knew where the drop was going to be."

Mel's mouth dropped open. "Jax was — was working with the FBI?"

"Yes. For a few months now. He came to them and offered to help put Jimmy away. We accepted and promised him a new life. Somewhere far away from this city."

Mel wiped at the tears that were starting to flow down her cheeks. "Too bad he's dead, huh? You didn't do a very good job of protecting your own fucking brother, did you?"

Jade winced and Cal squeezed her hand. "Mel, it's not like that."

"It is," she said dully. "Jax is dead and telling me that he actually was a good guy, doesn't make me feel any fucking better."

"Jax isn't dead," Cal said quietly.

She twitched all over and gave him an accusing look. "Don't, Cal. I'm tired of the fucking games."

"He isn't," Jade said. "We faked his death so that Jimmy would have to make the drop himself and we could arrest him. It was the only way to ensure that he went to prison for life. He needed to make the deal and the only way to do that was if both of his lieutenants were dead."

Mel stared blankly at her before switching her gaze to Cal. "He's dead, Cal. You told me two days ago, remember?"

He nodded solemnly. "I thought he was dead, Mel."

Jade leaned forward. "We faked his death, Mel. We put a bullet proof vest on him and one of our agents, pretending to be one of Chan's men, shot him in front of the grocery store. We put blood packs on him that burst on impact, and we planted another agent in the grocery store who posed as a doctor and pronounced him dead. He kept the civilians away from Jax until we could get his 'body' out of there."

"I don't understand what is happening," Mel whispered. "Why are you fucking with me like this?"

There was movement in the doorway and her gaze flickered upward. Cal made a soft noise of alarm as her face paled and her body swayed.

"Jax?" She whispered.

"Hello, butterfly."

She shook off Cal's hand and staggered to her feet before lurching toward him. She reached out with a trembling hand and touched his face. "You're alive."

"I am. I'm so sorry I lied to you, butterfly."

"You're alive," she repeated.

"Yes." He stroked her hair lightly and then flinched when she punched him in the stomach.

"You asshole!" She shouted before punching him again. "I thought you were dead! Do you have any idea what that did to me?"

"I'm sorry, I know I shouldn't have – "

"Jackass! Dickhead! Motherfucker!" She shouted before wrapping her hands around the back of his neck and yanking him downward.

"Bastard!" She muttered and kissed him fiercely.

He returned her kiss and after a moment Jade stood and gave Cal a pointed look. He followed her out of the room as Mel tore her mouth free and rested her forehead against Jax's.

"I hate you," she whispered.

"Liar," he replied.

He took her hand and led her to the table. "Sit down, butterfly. You're shaking like a leaf."

She nearly fell into the chair and he steadied her with his good hand as he sat down beside her. She reached out and touched his face lightly and he turned his head and kissed the palm of her hand.

"Tell me," she said. "Tell me everything."

* * *

"Wait," Court opened the bottle of beer and set it in front of Julie before opening his own. "He asked her to go into witness protection with him?"

"Yes," Cal said impatiently as he paced the spacious kitchen in Julie's house. "Pay attention, Courtney. Jesus! Jade and I convinced Jax that he needed to tell Melanie he was alive, to give her the chance to decide if she wanted to go with him. He told her the truth about everything and then asked her to disappear with him. She was so happy to realize he was alive that I thought they were just going to ride off into the fucking sunset together but she said no."

"She said no?" Julie set her beer bottle down with a surprised thump. "Really?"

"Yes, really! Jade and I were waiting in the living room for them and the next thing you know Mel comes flying out of the kitchen sobbing her eyes out, and leaves."

"I can't believe she said no," Julie said quietly.

"Why wouldn't she?" Court asked. "She barely knows the guy and he might be on the straight and narrow now but he worked for a drug dealer for nearly his entire life."

"He's a good guy, Court," Cal snapped. "Don't be so judgemental."

Court stared at him. "What has gotten into you, Cal?"

"What do you mean?"

"This is our baby sister you're talking about. Do you really want her disappearing from our lives, forever? What about mom and dad? What about us? I don't want to never see her again."

"I told you — it's not forever. A year, maybe two at the most. Jax will testify at the trial and then once the trial is over he promised Mel they would move back here."

"Cal, it's still a year of not talking to her, of not knowing if she is safe or happy or — "

"Jax makes her happy. I think she's in love with him and I know he's in love with her," Cal said.

"They aren't in love," Court said. "They barely know each other and – "

"Hello Mr. Pot," Julie said. "Have you met Mr. Kettle?"

"It's different with us, Jules," Court protested.

"No, it isn't," Julie said.

"That's why we need to do an intervention," Cal said.

"An intervention?" Court took a swig of his beer as Cal nodded anxiously.

"Yes, a love intervention!"

Court nearly spit beer all over the table. "Christ, Cal. Melanie's a grown woman, she doesn't need us interfering with her love life."

Julie frowned at him. "If it hadn't been for Mel doing a 'love intervention' with us, we wouldn't be together now, Court."

Court hesitated before setting his beer bottle down with a loud thump. "Shit, you're right."

He studied Cal for a moment. "You know mom and dad are going to kill us for talking her into this, right?"

"I do," Cal said. "It's worth it."

"Fine. Let's go." Court grabbed Julie's hand and pulled her up as Cal cheered loudly and followed them out of the kitchen.

* * *

"Let us in, Mel! We know you're in there!" Cal hollered before pounding on the door again.

"Maybe she isn't home," Julie said.

"She is! I know she is." He reached up to pound on the door again as Mel yanked it open.

"What the hell, Cal? It's late – are you trying to get the neighbours to call the cops?"

He pushed past her and with a soft sigh, Mel stepped back so that Court and Julie could follow him.

"We're here to do an intervention, Melanie Thomas," Cal said dramatically.

"An intervention?"

"Yes. A love intervention. Jax Anderson loves you and I know you love him too and you're making a huge mistake by just letting him walk away. If you don't go with him, you're going to regret it for the rest of your life and – "

"Cal," Court said.

Cal waved his hand irritably at him. "Not now, Court. I'm on a roll."

He grabbed Mel by the shoulders and shook her lightly. "You play it too safe, Mel. It's time you stopped looking after Court and me and lived your life. You deserve to be happy and – "

"Cal," Court repeated.

Ignoring him, Cal said, "You convinced Court that he was meant to be with Julie and you were right. Look how happy they are! You deserve that too and I think – "

"CALVIN!"

"What, Court? Christ, can't you see I'm trying to talk some sense into our sister?" Cal glared at him.

Court pointed behind him and Cal turned to see the two large suitcases sitting in the middle of the room. He gave Mel a puzzled look. "Mel? What's going on?"

"What does it look like?" Court said dryly. "Our love intervention isn't necessary."

Cal stared wide-eyed at Mel. "You're going with him?"

Mel nodded. "Yes. Well, I think I am. I mean, I did quit my job this morning, I called Jade and told her I changed my mind, and in the morning I'm going to mom's and dad's and breaking the news to them. Of course, I have exactly twenty-four hours to get my entire apartment packed up and moved into storage and that's not exactly going smoothly."

"We'll pack up your apartment and get your stuff to storage for you, honey," Julie said.

"We will?" Court asked.

Julie whacked him on the arm. "Yes, Court. We will."

"You mean you'll use your boatload of money to hire someone to come in and pack up her apartment for us, right?" Court said hopefully.

She laughed and he grinned at her and kissed her on the forehead as Cal threw his arms around Mel and hugged her hard.

"What did Jax say?" He asked.

"He doesn't know yet."

"What? Why not?"

"Because I still had to try and get my shit into storage and I still have to tell mom and dad. There's no guarantee that dad won't kidnap me and take me to the cabin once I tell them."

"Ooh, good point," Court said. "We'd better go with you. Safety in numbers, right? If he tries to kidnap you, Cal and I will distract him and give you time to escape."

Mel burst into laughter and hugged both Cal and Court. "Thanks, you guys. Really."

"That's what big brothers are for," Cal said.

* * *

"I'm going to miss you, Jade."

"It's only for a year, honey," she said.

They were standing on the airport tarmac and he studied the small plane before smiling faintly at her. "My own private jet, huh?"

"Only the best for the guy who helped bring Jimmy Golden down."

"Ricky and Lucy?" He asked.

She laughed. "Don't worry. Your babies are safe and sound and waiting for you on the plane."

"Good."

"You know you could have left them with me. I don't mind looking after them," she said.

"No, I want them with me. It's a long time without them," he said.

She smiled at him. "You'll be okay, Jax."

"Will you?"

"Of course I will," she said.

"Are you really going to prosecute him yourself?"

She shrugged. "I'm going to try. My superiors don't think it's a good idea and they think the judge assigned to the case won't let me. Too much of a conflict of interest."

"It kind of is," he said.

"It isn't," she insisted, "unless it's a conflict of interest that I hate his guts and will do whatever it takes to see him in prison for the rest of his life?"

He hugged her hard with his good arm. "I'm still worried."

"Don't be." She glanced at her watch and he arched his eyebrow at her.

"Do you have somewhere else to be?"

"As a matter of fact, I do," she said. "I have a date."

"With who?"

"No one you know," she said innocently.

"Jade..."

She grinned at him. "Cal Thomas."

"You're kidding."

"I'm not. He's mildly charming in an annoying kind of way," she laughed.

She hugged him tightly and kissed his cheek. "Go on, honey. Start your new life. Be happy, okay?"

"Okay. I love you, Jade."

"I love you too, Jax."

She watched as he climbed the stairs of the plane and stopped at the top. He turned and waved and she waved back before smiling to herself and walking to her car. She hoped he liked the surprise waiting for him in the plane.

Jax nodded to the air attendant standing by the door as she said, "Good evening, sir. Can I get you a drink?"

"No, thanks."

He moved into the main cabin and his jaw dropped. Mel was sitting in one of the leather chairs. Ricky and Lucy's crate was on the seat beside her and she had her fingers poked into the crate and was petting them gently.

"Hello, Jax." She smiled sweetly at him.

"Butterfly? What – what are you doing here?" He asked hoarsely.

"You invited me, remember?" She said teasingly as she stood and moved toward him.

"I – you said you couldn't go with me," he said.

"I changed my mind. And it's a good thing I did because Cal dragged Court and Julie over to my place for an emergency love intervention. Who knows how long it would have gone on if I hadn't already been packed."

"You changed your mind," he repeated.

"I did," she said.

"Why?"

"Does it matter?"

"No. Wait – what's a love intervention?"

She laughed loudly. "I'll explain later."

"But what about your job? Your family?" He asked.

"I quit my job yesterday and I told mom and dad this morning. They weren't exactly pleased but Court and Cal helped smooth it over. Besides, it's only a year or two and Jade gave me a secret email that I could use to email them. It's all very 'James Bond' like."

"Mel, are you – are you sure this is what you want to do?" He asked.

"I've never been more sure of anything in my life, Jax Anderson," she said quietly. "I want to be with you. Do you want to be with me?"

"Yes. God yes," he muttered before yanking her into his embrace and kissing her hard on the mouth.

"You won't regret this, butterfly. I promise you," he whispered against her mouth.

She kissed him again before smiling at him. "I know."

END

Please enjoy an excerpt from Ramona's novel,
"The Assistant".

THE ASSISTANT

By Ramona Gray

Copyright 2015 Ramona Gray

* * *

"Ms. Jones! My office, immediately."

His voice, harsh and demanding, spilled out of his office and I sighed before standing up from my desk. Smoothing my skirt, I entered his office and smiled at my boss.

"Is there a problem, Mr. Wright?"

"Shut the door," he barked.

I shut the door and sat down in one of the leather chairs across from his desk. I crossed my legs delicately and his eyes drifted to my short hemline before he glared at me.

"As a matter of fact, there is a problem. A rather large one."

I pasted my best 'what can I do to help' look on my face and folded my hands in my lap.

He raked his hand through his hair before his gaze dropped to my chest. "Your outfit, Ms. Jones."

My cheeks flamed immediately and I pulled self-consciously at my too-tight blouse. "Wh-what do you mean?"

"You know exactly what I mean, Ms. Jones." He leaned forward and folded his own hands on the top of his desk. "It isn't work appropriate. What do you have to say for yourself?"

"Laundry day," I whispered.

He frowned. "What?"

"It was laundry day yesterday and I didn't have any quarters for the washing machine." I cleared my throat nervously. "I didn't have anything else to wear."

I was nearly sweating with embarrassment. I had hemmed and hawed over my outfit this morning for half an hour but, left without much choice, had decided to just go for it. I knew what I looked like. The shirt was much too tight. It hugged my large breasts and clung to my curves and the skirt, well let's just say that bending over was not an option.

"How long have you worked for me, Ms. Jones?"

"Three years."

"I would think that after three years you'd have a better understanding of the office dress policy. Wouldn't you?"

My temper flared and I scowled at him. "I'm not breaking any rules. My skirt is well within the regulation length."

He scowled back. "Is it? Then explain why I got an eyeful of your garters when I walked by your desk. And I'll bet you a thousand dollars that the first deep breath you take, your buttons on that shirt pop open. Showing your tits is a definite infraction, Ms. Jones."

I gaped at him. "Did you just talk about my tits?"

He sat back in his chair and I watched wide-eyed as his hands moved to the buckle of his belt. "As I was saying, you've created a large problem and it's up to you to solve it."

As he was speaking, his hands were unbuckling, unbuttoning and unzipping.

A small gasp escaped my throat when he tugged his cock through the opening in his pants. It was long and thick and hard as a rock, and my mouth dried up as I watched him stroke it firmly.

"Come here and solve the problem, Ms. Jones," he commanded.

Like a woman in a dream, I rose to my feet and crossed around his desk. I couldn't take my eyes off of his cock and as moisture dampened my panties, I unconsciously rubbed my thighs together in an effort to quell the throbbing that was starting between my legs.

"On your knees, Ms. Jones." He rolled back his chair and I knelt obediently between his legs.

My mouth was in front of his cock now and I watched his hand slide up and down before he wound his other hand in my hair and pushed me toward the head of his cock.

"Open," he said firmly.

I opened my mouth and moaned in sheer delight when he guided his cock past my lips. I closed my mouth around his throbbing length, my stomach tightening with pleasure when I heard his harsh moan.

"Good girl," he whispered. He petted and stroked my hair as I sucked enthusiastically. His hips were rising in his chair and he was thrusting more firmly into my mouth. I made a soft humming noise and he groaned again before pulling on my hair.

"All of it. I want you to take all of it." He pushed on the back of my head and I took a deep breath and –

"Lina! Earth to Lina!"

I jerked and nearly fell off the stool I was sitting on. My hand twitched and the salad tumbled off my fork and landed with a wet splat on my shirt. I cursed loudly and mopped at the salad dressing with my napkin.

"What the hell were you thinking about, Lina?" My co-worker, Amanda, bit into her sandwich and stared curiously at me.

I blushed and continued to dab at the stain. "Nothing. Why?"

"You had a weird look on your face."

I shrugged. "I'm just tired. I didn't sleep well last night. Rex still isn't doing well and I was up half the night with him."

Amanda gave me a look of sympathy. "I'm sorry. I know how much he means to you."

"Thanks." I smiled at her and then glanced at the clock. "Shit. I've got to get back to my desk. Mr. Wright left a ton of documents for me before he went to his meeting. If I don't have them finished by the time he gets back, he'll have my head."

Amanda rolled her eyes. "I have no idea how or why you put up with him. He's an asshole."

I shrugged. "I need the money. It's not like there are a ton of jobs out there right now."

"I'd rather work at McDonalds then be his assistant," Amanda replied. "Do you know that before you, he went through seven assistants in just as many months? It was a bloodbath. I mean, we knew it would be difficult when Helen retired but seriously, we had no idea. The one girl had a nervous breakdown at her desk and Fran had to drive her home."

I laughed. "He's not that bad."

Amanda raised her eyebrow and I nodded in defeat. "Fine. He's that bad."

"Handsome bastard, though," Amanda said thoughtfully.

A snippet of my daydream reared its ugly head and I closed my eyes briefly before clearing my throat. "I hadn't noticed."

"Bullshit," Amanda scoffed.

"Fine. I've noticed. But honestly, he's such a douchebag that he isn't handsome to me anymore." There was no way in hell I would ever, even under the threat of hot needles being poked under my nails, admit to my crush on my asshole boss.

I slid off the stool and pulled nervously at my top and skirt. "Hey, Amanda? What do you uh, think of my outfit today?"

Amanda eyed me critically. "You look good. Different, but good." She hesitated. "Your shirt might be a teensy too tight for the office."

"Yeah," I sighed. "It's laundry day."

Amanda laughed and popped a grape into her mouth. "I overheard Gary and Marvin discussing your breasts by the photocopier machine. Gary thinks you're a D cup but Marvin is confident you're a double D."

"Fucking perverts," I muttered.

"They sure are," Amanda agreed cheerfully. "So, which is it? D or double D?"

I stuck my tongue out at her. "None of your business, Pervey McPerve."

She laughed again. "You should have seen the looks on their faces when they turned around and saw Mr. Wright standing behind them."

I groaned. "Please tell me he didn't overhear them."

"Of course he did. He gave them that look - you know the one - and told them if they had enough time to discuss their co-worker's assets over the water cooler, then he obviously wasn't giving them enough clients. Next thing you know, they're both buried in files."

She snorted laughter as I tugged again at my top and left the lunch room.

* * *

I sighed wearily and rubbed my aching back before bending over the filing cabinet in Mr. Wright's office. It was close to seven and I was tired and hungry. The building was empty and I kicked off my shoes as I stuffed files back into the cabinet.

Technically I didn't have to work late, Mr. Wright hadn't even returned to the office this afternoon, but my day tomorrow would be much smoother if I did. Besides, I wanted to leave a little early tomorrow. Rex had yet another vet appointment and it would be much easier to get Mr. Wright to agree if I was caught up on my work.

I glanced around his office as I grabbed another file folder. I hated being in here. It smelled like him, like the expensive cologne he always wore, and I swear to God some days I could smell it even at my apartment. Not surprising. Most days I spent more time in here than I did at my own desk. Of course his cologne would linger on me.

I grabbed another folder and bent over the filing cabinet again. I was just sliding it into its proper spot when his low voice spoke directly behind me.

"Working late, Ms. Jones?"

I yelped in surprise and straightened, my hands rushing to pull my skirt into a more appropriate position. He was so close I could feel his breath on the back of my neck, and I twitched in surprise when I felt his erection brush against my ass.

"No, don't." His hands pulled mine away from my skirt and I gasped when he let his fingers stroke my nylon-clad thigh. "You didn't strike me as a garters and thong kind of girl, Ms. Jones."

"I – a girl has to have a few surprises, Mr. Wright," I squeaked out.

"Indeed. Go on, finish your filing," he instructed.

Holding the folder between my suddenly sweaty fingers, I tried to move past him. He made a noise of disapproval and his hands curled around my waist. "I think you can reach it from here, Ms. Jones."

I took a deep breath and bent over, stretching to put the folder away as his hands moved from my waist to my hips. My skirt was riding up and he helped it along with a few firm tugs. I moaned quietly when his hard hands stroked my ass and his finger tugged at the silk between my cheeks.

"Your skirt is much too short for the office, Ms. Jones. You're not setting a very good example for the other secretaries," he chided sternly as his hands continued to rub and caress.

"I'm sorry," I moaned.

"I don't believe you. I think you wore this skirt on purpose. I think you want me to punish you," he said silkily.

"Mr. Wright, I – "

His hand came down, smacking my backside sharply and I let out a squeal of protest.

"Quiet, Ms. Jones. Take your punishment like a good girl." His hand was sliding into my hair and when he pulled my head up and licked my throat, I thrust my ass against him. He spanked me again and I bit back my gasp of pain.

"Open your legs, Ms. Jones." His hand tightened in my hair and I parted my legs eagerly. His hand cupped me through the silk and I moaned loudly.

"You're not to enjoy this. Do you understand?" He said sternly.

"Yes," I whispered.

His fingers were working their way under my panties. "If you come, your punishment will be even more severe. Is that what you want?"

"No," I moaned. His fingers were almost there, they were nearly touching me and knowing that he would feel how wet I was only excited me more. I spread my legs wider and held my breath. If he didn't touch me, I would –

"Ms. Jones?"

I gave a startled shriek and straightened before whirling around. The object of my sexual fantasies was standing in the doorway of his office and, blushing furiously, I yanked my skirt down.

Oh God. I had just flashed my boss. There was no way in hell he hadn't seen my super-sized ass in my too-short skirt and while that might have been a-okay in my fantasies, it most certainly was not in real life. The plain white cotton underwear I was wearing wasn't turning anyone on any time soon.

"What are you doing in my office?" He frowned at me as he strode toward his desk. He was still wearing his suit but he had loosened his tie and unbuttoned the first few buttons of his shirt.

"Filing."

"Obviously," he snapped. "I meant, why are you still here? It's late."

I shrugged. "I wanted to get it finished before I left."

"Your dedication to your job is admirable." There was a tone of sarcasm in his voice and I scowled at him.

"You know, most bosses would be impressed by their assistant's dedication."

"Indeed." He sank into his chair and pulled a glass and a bottle of scotch from the bottom drawer. "Or perhaps they would hope that their secretary was capable of getting her job done during regular working hours."

I bit back my smart-ass retort. I hated being called his secretary and the man knew it. It was a dated and ridiculous term and he used it solely to get under my skin. Normally I would call him on it but I still needed to leave early tomorrow.

I quickly filed the last folder and slipped into my shoes as he poured scotch into a glass. He opened his laptop and stared moodily at the screen as I approached his desk and cleared my throat.

"What is it, Ms. Jones?"

"I need to leave early tomorrow."

"For what purpose?" He gave me a sharp glance.

"I have an appointment."

He frowned at me. "You've had a lot of appointments as of late."

I didn't reply. I had never mentioned Rex to him. Mr. Wright didn't strike me as a dog lover and I wouldn't put it past him to deny my request just because he hated dogs.

He took a swallow of his scotch. "Fine."

"Thank you, Mr. Wright."

"Good night, Ms. Jones," he replied dismissively.

I rolled my eyes and closed his door before collapsing in the chair at my desk. I had worked for Aiden Wright for three years. Three years of putting up with his shit, his sarcasm, his crazy work demands. Three years of crying in the bathroom and watching my social life go down the drain because of my work schedule. I shook my head and collected my stuff before moving to the elevators. The other financial advisors gave their assistants flowers and took them for lunch on Administrative Assistant Day. They gave bonuses at Christmas and never called them in from their vacation because they needed a document typed. In the three years I had worked for him, Aiden Wright had never once given me a bonus or hell, even told me I was doing a good job. I was a fool to keep working for him.

So why are you? Find another job where you're not treated like dirt.

It was excellent advice and one that I would never follow. Some weird part of me liked the constant stress working for Aiden Wright caused. The thought of sitting in some office where my boss was always perfectly polite and perfectly reasonable, made me want to break out in hives. I hated to be bored and working for Mr. Wright was far from boring.

Whatever. You just keep hoping all your goddamn sexual fantasies about the man will come true someday.

My cheeks reddened and I stepped out of the elevator in a hurry. I crossed the lobby, my heels clicking loudly in the silence, and walked quickly to my car. It was freezing cold and I cursed loudly when I slipped and nearly landed on my ass.

The man is not attracted to fat girls. Get it through your head, you idiot.

I sighed and rubbed my hands together briskly as I waited for my car to warm up. Aiden Wright was sex on a stick. His dark hair and dark eyes, the sharp cheekbones and the perfect amount of stubble that always covered his jaw, made women drool. He worked out religiously every morning in the gym in the basement of our office building and at 6'4" he towered over nearly every one.

I sighed again and drove out of the parking lot. My fantasies about my boss had to stop. They had really heated up over the last few days and although part of me knew it was a coping mechanism for the stress, it was time to end them. Although I had never once seen Mr. Wright with a woman, I knew without a doubt that I wasn't his type. Besides, he was probably the type of guy who liked a woman to be in control in bed.

I snorted out loud as I drove carefully down the icy streets. That was complete and utter bullshit and I knew it. Mr. Wright was a man who demanded obedience and there was no reason to think he wouldn't be the same in the bedroom. Fresh wetness dampened my panties at the thought of being under his control and I groaned and slammed my hand against the steering wheel. I really needed to get laid.

* * *

Follow Ramona on Twitter or Facebook for updates and release date information or sign up for her monthly newsletter on her website.

If you would like more information about Ramona Gray, please visit her at:

www.ramonagray.ca
or
https://www.facebook.com/RamonaGrayBooks
or
https://twitter.com/RamonaGrayBooks

Books by Ramona Gray

Printed in Great Britain
by Amazon